"A master doing what he does best . . . [Coover] attains a grittily poetic quality reminding us of Cormac McCarthy at his best . . . splatter scenes with moments that take us to the core of existential American solitude."
— Sven Birkerts, *The New York Times Book Review*

"[A] fantastic fable— part myth, part comedy, part movie, part book . . . A crazy dream, so familiar and funny, such a steadfast cradle of a plot that Coover can just rock his characters to sleep in it, let his twinkling sentences wink and nod and nudge with only an ominous landscape for a God . . . makes the reader feel like a kid again."— *Los Angeles Times Book Review*

"Cunningly good-humored horseplay . . . a bewitching play of desire . . . [Coover's is] a literary career dedicated to combating reductive and linear thought, to subverting the inexorable logic that sends knight to princess, cowboy to sunset, or the Rosenbergs to the electric chair."— *The Times Literary Supplement* (London)

"*Ghost Town* might be billed as the first phantasmagorical western. . . . There are those among us who find the works of William Gaddis, William Gass, John Barth, Thomas Pynchon, John Hawkes and others of this group of middle-age Northern and Midwestern WASPs to be more fun to discuss as theory than to read. . . . Coover, though, also possesses gifts more associated with traditional fiction. One of them is an ear for American idiom utterly lacking in the writers he's often grouped with."
— *Chicago Tribune*

"An end-of-the-century, postmodern western that turns just about every one of the genre's clichés inside out and upside down, and in the process, reconstitutes one of America's most enduring myths (that of the lone western hero) into a ribald fantasy. . . . It hits the mark dead on, leaving the reader feeling this was the way the Old West really was."— *Booklist*

"In apparent acknowledgement of the fact that reading requires the same type of self-deluding participation as witnessing a daredevil 'risk' death—or letting your imagination run wild in a ghost town—postmodern authors like Coover want to lift the scales from our eyes, rarely allowing us to forget we are being lied to and played with. . . . [*Ghost Town*] reads like a hallucination . . . lovely, lyrical."—*The Philadelphia Inquirer*

"Justly prized among America's foremost innovations in fiction, Robert Coover's novels have wickedly parodied tried-and-true genres, like films, fairy tales and bedtime stories, with vertiginous linguistic energy and outrageously nasty fun. . . . The punch of *Ghost Town* lies in its hallucinatory quality and its sense of fair play . . . giving us a truer, more visceral sense of the West's hyperbolic cavils and redneck cruelties."—*The Seattle Times*

"Beautiful . . . The irony of Robert Coover's slender new novel, *Ghost Town*, is that even though it is fiction, [*Ghost Town*] feels like coming home. . . . This is the West of John Wayne written in magic-realist ink, and it is very good."—*The Economist*

WORKS BY ROBERT COOVER

Short Fiction
PRICKSONGS AND DESCANTS
IN BED ONE NIGHT & OTHER BRIEF ENCOUNTERS
A NIGHT AT THE MOVIES

Plays
A THEOLOGICAL POSITION

Novels
GERALD'S PARTY
THE ORIGIN OF THE BRUNISTS
THE UNIVERSAL BASEBALL ASSOCIATION, INC.
J. HENRY WAUGH, PROP.
A POLITICAL FABLE
SPANKING THE MAID
WHATEVER HAPPENED TO GLOOMY GUS OF THE CHICAGO BEARS?
PINOCCHIO IN VENICE
JOHN'S WIFE
BRIAR ROSE
THE PUBLIC BURNING
GHOST TOWN

GHOST TOWN

GHOST TOWN

A NOVEL

Robert Coover

GROVE PRESS
New York

First published in hardcover in 1998 by Henry Holt and Company, Inc.,
New York.

Published simultaneously in Canada
Printed in the United States of America

Portions of *Ghost Town* first appeared in *Conjunctions, Marvels & Tales,
Journal of Fairy-Tale Studies*, and *Playboy*.

FIRST GROVE PRESS EDITION

Library of Congress Cataloging-in-Publication Data
Coover, Robert.
Ghost town : a novel / Robert Coover.
p.   cm.
ISBN 0-8021-3666-4
1. Frontier and pioneer life—West (U.S.)—Fiction. 2. Cowboys—West
(U.S.)—Fiction.
I. Title.

PS3553.O633 G48 2000
813'.54—dc21   99-051708

Designed by Kelly Soong

Grove Press
841 Broadway
New York, NY 10003

00 01 02 03   10 9 8 7 6 5 4 3 2 1

For: Joe Aulisi, George Bamford, Alice Beardsley, Beeson Carroll, John Coe, Steve Crowley, Cherry Davis, Jack Gelber, Bob Gunton, Wynn Handman, Grania Hoskins, Sy Johnson, Franklin Keysar, Kert Lundell, Julia Miles, Roger Morgan, Jenny O'Hara, Albert Ottenheimer, Caymichael Patten, Neil Portnow, Don Plumley, David Ramsey, James Richardson, Dale Robinette, Edward Roll, and Stanley Walden.

Youpy ti yi youpy youpy yea.

GHOST TOWN

Bleak horizon under a glazed sky, flat desert, clumps of sage, scrub, distant butte, lone rider. This is a land of sand, dry rocks, and dead things. Buzzard country. And he is migrating through it. Because: it is where he is now, and out here there's nothing to stop for, no turning back either, nothing back there to turn to. His lean face is shaded from the sun overhead by a round felt hat with a wide brim, dun-colored like the land around, old and crumpled. A neckerchief, probably once red, knotted around his throat, collects what sweat, in his parched saddle-sore state, he sweats. A soft tattered vest, gray shirt, trail-worn cowhide chaps over dark jeans tucked into dust-caked boots with pointed toes, all of it busted up and threadbare and rained on, dried out by sun and wind and grimed with dust, that's the picture he makes, forlorn horseman on the desert plain, obstinately plodding along. He wears a wooden-butted six-shooter just under his ribs, a bowie knife with a staghorn handle in his belt, and a rifle dangles, barrel aimed at his partnering shadow on the desert floor, from the saddle horn. He is leathery and sunburnt and old as the hills. Yet just a kid. Won't ever be anything else.

It wasn't always like this. There were mountains before, a rugged and dangerous terrain, with crags and chasms, raging rivers in deep gorges, and dense forests, unsociably inhabited. He's known snakebites, mountain lion and wolfpack attacks, blizzards and thunderstorms, frostbite, windburn, gnats and locusts and mosquitoes, grizzlies too, cinch bugs, arrow wounds—a black-haired scalp, hair braided with shells and beads, is strung from his gunbelt, though if asked he couldn't say where it came from, just something that happened, must have. Back then, he was maybe chasing someone or something. Or was being chased, some vague threat at his back, that's mostly what he remembers now from that time, an overwhelming feeling of danger, or else of despair, that filled the air whenever the sky darkened or the trail petered out. He had to bury someone on one occasion, as he recalls, someone like a brother, only the dead man in the hole he'd dug wasn't really dead but kept moving blindly, kicking the dirt away, in fact he was himself the one who kept twisting and turning, the one blindly kicking, he was down in the burial pit with dirt peppering his face, but then he wasn't again, and the one who was was crawling out suddenly to flail at the air, flesh sliding off the bone like lard off a hot pan; so he left that place, to go chase someone, or to be chased, or finally just to move on to somewhere else, not to see things like that.

Then one day, climbing up out of a steep canyon cut by a wild frothy river way down below, struggling all the while against some kind of unseen force pressing down on him, almost palpable, as if a big flopping bird were expiring on his chest, having to dismount finally and haul his shying wild-eyed horse up through the last fierce pass, he found himself out upon this vast empty plain, where nothing seems to have happened yet and yet everything seems already over, done before begun. A space there and not there, like a monumental void, dreadful and ordinary all at once. As if the ground the horse treads, for all its extension, might be paper thin and stretched over nothing. He doesn't expect to come to the end of the world out here, but he doesn't expect not to.

What he's aiming at is a town over on the far horizon, first thing he saw when he rose up out of the canyon and the canyon shut itself away behind him. The town's still out there, sitting on the edge like a gateway to the hidden part of the sky. Sometimes it disappears behind a slight rise, then reappears when that rise is reached, often as not even further away to the naked eye, his naked eye, than when last seen, like a receding mirage, which it likely is. Sometimes there's no horizon at all, burned away by the sun's glare or night's sudden erasure, so no town either, and his goal is more like the memory of a goal, but he keeps moving on and sooner or later it shows itself again, wavering in the distance as if made of a limp sheet that the wind was ruffling. He doesn't know what it's rightly called, nor feels any need to know. It's just the place he's going to.

Maybe he dozes off betweentimes, but out here it seems always to be either dark and starcast or else the sun is directly overhead, beating down on him as though fingering him for some forgotten crime, just one condition or its contrary like the two pictures on a magic lantern slide, flickering back and forth, as he opens and closes and opens his eyes. Nothing much could sneak up on him in all this emptiness as long as he's mounted above it, so in the saddle is where he does most of his sleeping, his eating too, which is largely confined to the strips of old buffalo jerky, black as tar and half as tasty, that came with the horse. He could use a watering hole, a bit of forage for the beast between his legs, the best prospects for which would seem to be that town on the horizon, unsubstantial though it appears. Out here, nothing but stumpy cactus and tumbleweeds and a few old dry bones, provender unfit for the dead.

Who haunt him, or seem to, whispering at his back like a dry wind with eyes. That feeling of eyes in the air gets so potent at times that he has to stretch round in his saddle to cast his gaze on what's behind him, and one day, bent round like that, he discovers another town on the opposite horizon, a kind of mirror image of the one he's headed toward, as if he were coming from the same place he was going. A vapor of the atmosphere, he supposes, but the next time he looks it's back there still and clearer than it was before, as if it might be gaining on him. Which is the case, for as the days, if they are days, go on, the town behind him closes upon him even as the one in front recedes, until at last it glides up under his horse's hoofs from behind and proceeds to pass him by even as he ambles forward. He tries to turn his horse around to face this advent, but the creature's course is set and it is clearly past considering further instruction. It's a plain town that comes past, empty and silent, made of the desert itself with a few ramshackle false-fronted frame structures lined up to conjure a street out of the desolation. Nothing moves in it. In an open window, a lace curtain droops limply, ropes dangle lifelessly from the gallows and hitching posts, the sign over the saloon door hangs heavy in the noontime sun as the blade of an ax. A water trough catches his eye as it drags lazily by, and he spurs the horse forward, but he cannot seem to overtake it. The whole dusty street heaves lazily past like that, leaving him soon at the edge of town and then outside it. He halloos once at the outskirts, but without conviction, and gets no reply, having expected none. He is alone again on the desert. The town slowly slips away ahead of him and grows ever more distant and finally vanishes over the horizon and night falls.

☙ ☙ ☙

There's a dull flickering light on the desert floor as if a decaying star has slipped from its rightful place, and he follows it to a warmthless campfire where a group of men huddle under serapes and horse blankets, smoking and drinking and chewing, bandits by the look of them.

Look whut the cat drug in, one of them says, and spits into the low flame.

Reckon it's human?

Might be. Might not. Turd on a stick, more like.

He's just stood in his stirrups to ease himself out of the saddle, but he changes his mind and rests back down. A tin pot squats at the edge of the smoldering fire, leaning into it as though in mockery of the squatting men and emitting a burnt coffee stink that mingles unfavorably with the viscid reek of burning dung.

It dont make a damn t'me, says another, without looking up from under the wide floppy hat brim that covers his lowered face, lest I kin neither eat it nor fuck it.

Dont look much good fer one'r tother. Lest mebbe it's one a them transvested pussies.

Y'reckon? Little shitass dont look very beardy at thet.

C'mere, kid. Bend over'n show us yer credentials.

Ifn they aint been down outa thet saddle in a spell, I misdoubt I wishta witness em.

The men hoot damply and expectorate some more. Whut's yer game, kid? the one under the floppy hat asks into the fire, his voice gravelly and hollow like one erupting from a fissure in the earth deep below him. Whuddayu doin out here?

Nuthin. Jest passin through.

That also seems to amuse them all for some reason. Lordy lordy! Jest passin through!

Ifn thet dont beat all!

A one-eyed mestizo in a rag blanket lifts a buttock and farts fulminously. Sorry, boys. Thet one wuz jest passin through.

Just as well to keep moving on, he figures, and to that purpose he gives his mustang a dig in the flanks, but the horse drops its head in solemn abjuration, inclined, it seems, to go no further.

So whar yu passin through to, kid? asks a wizened graybeard in filthy striped pants, red undershirt, and a rumpled derby. Next to him, the man in the floppy hat is deftly rolling shredded tobacco into a thin yellow leaf between knotty fingers.

Thet town over thar. His rifle is off the saddle horn now and resting on his thighs.

Yu dont say.

Wastin yer time, boy. Nuthin over thar.

Then nuthin'll hafta do.

Yu'll never git thar, kid.

Aint nuthin but a ghost town.

I'll git thar.

Hunh!

Ifn they's any gittin to be done, son, says the graybeard in red skivvies and derby, I'd advise yu t'rattle yer hocks outa the Terrortory and trot em back home agin. Pronto.

Caint do thet.

No? Floppy hat licks the tobacco leaf, presses it down. Why not, kid? Whar yu from?

Nowhars.

Nobody's from nowhars. Who's yer people?

Aint got none.

Everbody's got people.

I aint.

Thet's downright worrisome. The man tucks the thin yellow tube away under the overhanging hat brim at the same time that a tall ugly gent in a flat-crowned cap, much punctured, and with stiff tangled hair spidering down to his hairy shirt, stuffs a fresh chaw into his jaws and asks him what's his mustang's name.

Thet's it.

Whut's it?

Mustang.

Shit, thet aint nuthin of a name. He spits a gob against the tin pot to fry it there.

Dont need no other.

Dont fuck with me, son. Hoss must have a proper name.

Ifn he does, he never tole it to me.

Thet boy's a real smartass, aint he?

Either him or the hoss is.

Tell me, kid, says floppy hat, holding an unstruck match out in front of his fresh-made cigarillo. And I dont want no shit. Dont keer fuck-all about the damn hoss. But whut's yer name?

Caint rightly say. Whut's yers?

We call him Daddy Dunne, says a grizzled hunchback with greasy handlebars sloping to his clavicle like a line drawing of the shadowy deformity behind his ears. On accounta he dont do no more. And they all laugh bitterly again, all except the man under discussion, who is lighting up.

So why dont yu git down off thet mizzerbul critter'n come set with us a spell, says the one-eyed mestizo, unsmiling.

He watches them without expression, knowing what must come next, even while not knowing where that knowing has come from.

Y'know, says a scrawny skew-jawed wretch, pulling on his warty nose, thet young feller dont seem over friendly.

Looks like he's plumb stuck on thet dang animule.

Looks like he's hitched to it.

Lissen, boy. I ast yu a question, floppy hat says, straightening up ever so slightly, so the glowing tip of his cigarillo can be seen in the voided dark beneath the broad brim, both hands braced like talons on his knees.

The rider shifts his seat for balance, his finger edging up the rifle stock toward the trigger, and in the fallen hush the saddle creaks audibly like a door suddenly opening under him. And I done answered it, ole man, he says.

Nobody moves. There is a long direful stillness during which a wolf howls somewhere and stars fall in a scatter, streaking across the domed dark like flicked butts. Then that dies out, too, and everything stops. It goes on so long, this star-stunned silence, it starts to feel like it won't ever not go on. As if time had quit on them and turned them all to stone. The rider, the horse under him gone rigid and cold, feels his own heart winding down. Only his hands have any action left in them. He uses them, struggling against the torpor that fetters him, to raise his rifle barrel and shoot the man in the floppy hat. The impact explodes into the man's chest and his hat flies off and his mouth lets go the cigarillo and he pitches backwards onto the desert floor. With that, things ease up somewhat, the mustang snorting and shifting under him, the skies awhirl once more, the others watching him warily but returned to an animate state, more or less. Chewing. Spitting.

Yu shouldna done thet, kid, grumbles the ugly man with the spidery hair.

He rests the rifle back on his thighs again. Warnt my fault. He shoulda drawed.

Shit, sumbitch warnt even armed.

He's blind, kid. Stark starin.

Wuz.

The man he's shot lies arms asprawl on the desert floor, staring up at the night sky with eyes, he sees, as white as moons.

Yu shot an ole unarmed blind man, son. Whuddayu got t'say fer yerself?

He walks his horse over to the dead man, bends down from the saddle, and picks up the fallen cigarillo. Not a bandit, as he'd supposed, after all. Wearing a sheriff's badge, the star pierced by his rifle shot and black with blood. Probably he should shoot them all. Maybe they expect him to. Instead, he tucks the half-spent cigarillo between his cracked lips, sucks on it to recover the glow, and, without a backward glance, quits their wearisome company and slowly rides away.

It is high noon, and the main street of the vaporous town which has been so long eluding him now rolls up under his mustang's plodding hoofs as though in abrupt repair of some mechanical disorder. The street, with its dilapidated gray frame buildings squared off against the boundless desolation, is empty and silent and yet full of dimly heard echoes, a remote disturbance of mumbling voices, swept into town perhaps by the hot desert wind. A saloon sign creaks desultorily in this talking wind, frayed strands of hitching-rail rope turn idly, a lace curtain flutters in an open window. Particles of dust gather into airy spirals that dance in the street like hanged men with their arms tied behind them and as soon dissolve and then as soon regather to wind about again.

He dismounts and leads his horse past an old buckboard with a broken wheel to the water trough. Nothing but a dry dust bed in its tin hollow. At one end by a bowed porch column he finds a well pump with a rusty handle, gives it a crank. No resistance. Like wagging a dead man's bones. Under the saloon sign overhead, a small board hangs by knotted cords with the word ROOMS on it, though it's the crudely lettered COLD BEER notice tacked up over the doorway that most gets his attention. Rifle in hand, he steps through the swinging doors into the saloon's dense murk, ready for whatever, but whatever doesn't happen. The place is dark and empty, hotter inside than out. There's a scatter of tipped chairs and tables, broken lamps, a few empty dust-caked bottles lying about, but nothing with which to tickle the throat. An old grand piano, one of its legs caved in, sits on its haunches in one corner, baring its wide grinning row of yellowing teeth, its broken wires sprouting wildly like hair standing on end. A cobwebbed staircase leads up to the dim suggestion of the advertised rooms. No promise there, and that low muttering hum is worse in here, the way the wind is blowing through the shattered windows maybe, so he strolls back out into the glare, sand crunching under his boots on the board floors.

His horse has wandered away toward the edge of town. He can see it far off, head down, rear to the wind. Looking for water probably. He heads that way but is distracted by a sign painted on the crusted window of an old frame building: GOLD! it says. CLAIMS OFFICE. The door hangs loose on its sprung hinges. Inside, there's a wooden swivel chair and rolltop desk behind a counter, all blanketed by thick dust laid down over time, and on the counter a stack of cards with the sign: TAKE ONE. He takes the lot, turns them over: a pack of ordinary playing cards, but with coordinates of some kind inked onto each of their faces. He pockets the jack of spades, flings the others at the desk to make the dust erupt, steps back out onto the street.

The mustang has drifted further away, almost out of sight. He tries to whistle it back but his mouth is too dry, so he sets off after it once more, cursing it under his breath. The dusty wind tugs at his hat brim and flaps his raggedy vest in brief irregular gusts, and the horse keeps moving as he moves. Like he's trying to suck him out of this place. Or into trouble. He watches himself as though from high above as he strides down this scorched street of derelict banks and saloons, hardware, dry goods, and grocery stores, stables and brothels, laid out on the desert floor like two parallel lines drawn on a slate for the practice of handwriting, his passage the looped, crossed, and dotted text inscribed between, signifying nothing, and he is reminded at this high remove of something a lawman once told him in ancient times. Livin a life out here is shit, son. It's got no more meanin than writin in the sand with yer dick when the wind's up. To keep goin on, knowin that, sufferin that, is plain stupid. Loco, in fact. But to keep goin on, in the face a such shit, a such futility and stupidity and veritable craziness—that, son, *that* is fuckin suh-*blime*.

This high-minded overview is disrupted and he is brought swiftly down to earth again and back behind his own two eyes, when before those eyes appears, behind a dust-grimed window of a house well beyond the town center, a beautiful woman, very pale, dark hair done up in a tight bun, dressed all in black and staring out at him, as though in judgment, or else in longing. He pauses, holding on to his rifle and hat out there in the middle of the gusty street, transfixed by the inviolable purity of her framed visage, like something dreamt and come to life; but as, in a daze, he steps toward her, she fades back out of sight. He peers in through the window when he reaches it, face to the glass and cupped hand for an eyeshade: a barren room sparsely furnished with a couple of long midget-sized tables and a dozen straightback chairs with their legs sawed down, long since out of use. No sign of the woman. If any woman. Likely not. No more likely than that murmurous drone in his head is really carried on the fitful wind. It's that damned sun plaguing him. Still as directly overhead as when first he rode in.

No sign of his horse now either, nothing but another spectral dust devil coming and going where he saw him last. Although in such utter solitude he cannot figure where such a thought might come from, he thinks his horse may have been stolen, or might have allowed itself to be. But then he spies the perverse creature again, back by the saloon, near the buckboard, nosing once more the empty trough. Must have circled back when he wasn't looking. He calls to him and the horse looks up at him with a stricken expression, then turns away again. He walks back toward him, boots hurting him now, but the wind gusts briefly, curtaining the street with flying dust, and when it settles the horse is gone again. In its stead, in the sunbaked distance, four or five horsemen come riding in at a slow canter, dust popping in tiny explosions under their horses' hoofs, giving them the impression of approaching on

13

smutched clouds. They pull up at the saloon in dead silence, dismount into their own shadows, hitch their animals to the rail there, and, the tread of their boots on the wooden sidewalk unheard as if they trod on goose feathers, disappear through the swinging doors. Though he knows full well that no good can come of it, he follows them on in.

✧   ✧   ✧

In the saloon, men are clapping shoulders, shooting craps, drinking, laughing, brawling. Heard through the foggy racket: the soft slap of dealt cards, the *poytt! thupp!* of missed spittoons, the *rickety-click* of roulette and fortune wheels. Hit me, says a mustachioed fat man in a straw boater and raps his tabled cards with a balled-up fist. Beer is drawn. An ear is torn off. A bony bald man in a white shirt, yellow suspenders, and black string tie bangs out a melody on the grand piano, against which a buxom rouged-up lady with wild orange curls leans, singing a song about a good girl who went bad. She is dressed, like someone else he's seen today, all in black, except for the crimson ruffles on her blouse, a ruby pin worn in her pierced cheek like a beauty mark, and a brass key, shiny as gold, dangling between her powdered breasts on a black ribbon. The fat man in the boater takes a punch and careens backwards toward the piano player, who keeps his left hand going while raising his right elbow to deliver a hammer blow that sends the fat man caroming headfirst into the wall and nearly through it. THIS IS A SQUARE HOUSE says a sign over his head. The other cardplayers pick the fat man's pockets and divvy up his winnings.

I'm gonna kill thet fuckin humpback, someone breathes in his ear.

Who—?

Yer throw, podnuh.

There's a shot, and somewhere a horse whinnies as though in sudden terror.

Shitfire, parson! And I mean thet sincerely!

Shet yer gob'n git yer money down, yu ole dildock!

Awright, smack yu double, jughaid. So dole away!

Yu gonna roll them damn bones, son, or eat em? he's asked. A small circle of angry men glare up at him over their wild face hair, their pocked noses aglow under the kerosene lamp.

All he wants is a beer, anything wet, but the leather cup his hand has closed around holds only a pair of ivory dice. Across the barroom, the singer is dolefully lamenting the unlucky gambler who bet and lost, one by one, all his body parts. He rattles the cup of dice. She's hurtin tonight, he hears someone say behind him. Probly makes her peculiar hot, muses another. Yu reckon?

Whoa boy, a squint-eyed stringy-haired oldtimer in a gambler's knee-length black broadcloth coat cautions: Whut's yer stake here? Having none other, he tosses his hat down, gives the cup another shake, throws a natural, and wins all their hats. There's some grumbling. The oldtimer, scowling suspiciously, spins the dice on their corners while fingering an ebony-handled derringer tucked in his vest pocket.

He hooks his thumb in his belt, within reach of his own pistol. Just in case. Any a them hats wuth a beer? he asks, and they all snort at that and throw them at him in disgust.

A row is brewing meanwhile over behind the piano by the slowly spinning wheel of fortune. It's the man with the ear ripped off. I'm tired a yu blowin off at the mouth_so, he barks, blood cascading down the side of his head like a waterfall down a cliff face, and the baggy-eyed halfbreed he's addressing sends a thick smear toward a spittoon and says: They's a lotta truth in thet. Thet's yer lookout, mister, says the man with the ear gone, and pulls a sawed-off pistol out of his pants and shoves it up the halfbreed's broad brown nose. Before he can pull the trigger, though, the bald piano player, in the long perilous beat between chorus and verse (the lady is into a love song now about some legendary hero who was suddenly expired by an itinerant gunman and was "gone off to his reward, bless his big pointy boots"), rises up and head-butts him. The one-eared man's head splits with a pop as a clay bowl might and his brains ooze out like spilled oatmeal when he hits the floor, by which time the next verse has commenced and the piano player's back on his stool again. No one pays much attention to any of this.

Come back, cowboy, and do us like yu done before, moans the chanteuse, but more to the smoke-smudged ceiling, stretched out on the broad piano as she is now with the men of the saloon lining up and taking their turns on her. Through the jostle and the saloon's pearly light he can see she's wearing black petticoats and, flagged to one bobbing ankle, black drawers.

Seems like widow weeds is in fashion here, he remarks to the barkeep in a friendly manner, forcing a smile onto his parched lips.

The barkeep grunts. Here, they always is. He's a tall skinny man with stiff greasy hair reaching to his shoulders, making it look like an ugly insect is standing there, its belly resting on the top of his head. So whut kin I do yu fer, stranger?

Whuskey. Double. Not what he wants at all. What he craves is a few gallons of water. But he figures some things you can get in here and some you probably can't.

The tall ugly barkeep glares down at him, both hands braced on the bar edge, jerks his head inquiringly, making his locks walk about. Ah. He offers him the black flat-crowned hat full of holes he's just won off the oldtimer, best of the lot for all the damage to it, but the barkeep shakes it off. A truly formidable thirst has him by the throat and he's ready to barter away anything he's got, down to his weapons and his horse, assuming the horse is still in the neighborhood. Then he remembers the card from the claims office and he slaps it down on the bar.

There's a sudden hush. The barkeep backs away a step, hands fallen to his sides. The lady on the piano is sitting up, black skirts around her waist, and the men are stealthily pulling their breeches back on. The piano player sits stonily with his hands in his lap, staring at him, as do the faro, craps, and monte players, all hands poised. At the back, the tall fortune wheel creaks and ticks in its slow ceaseless rounds.

Who is thet kid? he hears someone whisper, though no lips move.

Some gunslinger most like.

Y'reckon?

Lookit thet injun scalp hangin from his belt!

But he's jest a brat. And he aint got but one pistol.

Thet we kin *see.*

Rifle, too. A blade . . .

The buggy-haired barkeep, who seems to have shrunk half a foot, sets a double shotglass on the bar and, his hand trembling, smiling a nervous gold-toothed smile, pours it full to overflowing. Before he can pick it up, though, the glass is batted away. It's the one-eared man with the oozing brains, back on his feet again. Whar'd yu git thet card, stranger? he asks, breaking the deathly silence, weaving unsteadily back and forth beneath the overhanging gas lamp. Whar'd yu git thet black one-eared jack? Everybody's watching them. It wasn't his intention to draw notice to himself, but it seems hard not to in here. Gimme it, kid. Gimme thet card.

He shrugs. Hell, I dont give a keer. Here, yu kin have the damn thing.

Goddammit! bellows the man, rage flushing his face, both sides of the split. Out comes a dirk, the blade agleam in the yellow lamplight. I said I want thet black jack!

And I said yu kin have it.

Yu gonna gimme thet fuckin card, boy, or I gotta kill yu fer it?

Awright, he says, seeing how it is and bracing himself. The man lunges at him with the dirk, exposed brains wobbling like gray custard: he deflects the thrust and it slices clean through his tattered vest from sleeve hole to bottom hem. He whips his own bowie knife out and, as the one-eared man plunges forward again, buries the blade deep in his belly. The man staggers back, staring down in amazement and confusion at the staghorn handle protruding from his stomach, which slowly sucks it up until it vanishes entirely. Even the pierced shirt seems to mend itself behind the handle as it sinks inside. The man looks up at him around the cleft in his skull, grins crookedly, opens his mouth as though to taunt him, and blood bubbles out. His eyes roll up and he topples over on his back. Blood continues to trickle from his mouth. Then his lips part and the knife handle slowly emerges like a stiff tongue. The men in the saloon gather round to watch it come squeezing out, bending close as though trying to decipher a message in the rivulets of blood coursing through the staghorn grooves. Offered up to him is how it seems, a kind of gift, or challenge, which he accepts, taking hold of it and midwifing it out from the man's lips. Not easy. Like drawing out a knife buried deep in wood, as if the man were sucking on it or biting down. A fountain of blood follows upon the blade's withdrawal, making those crowded around gasp and fall back. He wipes the blood off on the dead man's flannel shirt, tucks it back in his belt, and turns again to the barkeep, who hands him a shiny brass key strung on a black velvet ribbon. He nods up the stairs. No thanks, he says, and hands the key back. Jest gimme a goddam drink. But the barkeep is gone, the bar as well, and the key he is poking forward is sliding into a door lock.

Awaiting him on a brocade-laid table inside the room is a tall mug of cold beer and a plate of eggs and beans on fried cornbread. He has such an extravagant need, these things, consumed afoot, go down like air, but they ease somewhat, if not his wants, at least his apprehensions—where such feasts appear, more may follow—and he feels his saddle-hammered spine loosen like an unstrung fiddle bow. The room is filled with heavy carved furniture, not from this place, the high-headboarded bed heaped with quilts and fancy coverlets, satiny paper hiding the rough walls, lace curtains aflutter in the open windows like hovering butterflies. Butterflies! He rubs his bristly sunburnt jaw. Damn. Hasn't reflected upon those peculiar creatures since he entered upon the desert. Which has been a bit like getting sick. For an interminable long time.

Behind a hand-painted dressing screen is a wooden tub full of sudsy hot water, meant, must be, for him. As all else here, that bed in time, with its inviting headboard like a saloon's false front. He unknots the braided scalp from his gunbelt, sets it, belt, gun, and knife on the table, against which his rifle already leans, then sits down on the plush seat of a high-backed chair to work his boots off, breathing through his mouth against the prodigious reek. In front of an oak-framed mirror there, he stands to peel away the rest, his shredded vest and old gray shirt, chaps and denims, and the foul blighted rags that were once a suit of underwear, seeing in the glass beneath the shadowing hat the scrawny ulcerated thing he is, scabbed and scarred, in general a most unwholesome sight, but one he shares with the pale dark-haired widow woman he has seen before, standing now behind him in the reflection and gazing with quiet awe and pity upon his stark condition.

He turns to face her but there is no one there. The room is empty as before. As, somehow, he had surmised.

He unties the red rag, sweat-blackened, from around his neck and, dressed only in his wide-brimmed hat, steps into the tub, his feet, so recently liberated, reveling in the emollient power of the steaming water, seasoned with bath salts whose aroma bespeaks a distant land, one where flowers grow, or grew. What brought those butterflies peculiarly to mind, may be. He stands there for a moment, letting his feet swell out, soaking up this newfound bliss, then squats to accustom his beat-up backside and privates to the heat, finally sinks in whole up to his chin, his eyelids dropping like iron shutters over his eyes, forcing their hard gaze inward toward the softer sensations that, like sudden family, embrace him all about.

The fragrant water is not completely still but, stirred perhaps by his own entry, seems to eddy around him as if he were being bathed in a rippling brook fed by hot springs, one that cleanses itself even as it cleanses him. He feels buoyed up, stroked by the fingering currents, fondled soapily from head to foot as if he were in the hands of some water nymph or an Indian princess, one who touches him in all the tenderest places, turning pain to sweet delight, skilled as such creatures of nature are in the art of healing with water, or so he's heard. He tries to open his eyes, can't, so surrenders to these silky caresses and takes them for what they seem to be and quite likely are, all the killings he's done and seen soon washed away by them, and just as soon forgotten, or nearly so. Rolling in the water to open all his crevices to its tender attentions, or hers (as he thinks of them), he feels the water well up into volumes like liquid thighs, rolling as he rolls, and with spongy patches in between and wet lips that kiss and tickle, stripping his mind and spirit pure as his body is, and as is hers, bare breasts soft as foam brushing him gently as the water streams about. No such things in this watery world as widow weeds, no weeds at all, for she, like he, like all beings in this happy valley with its genial clime, goes always naked, stark staring, as someone's said, wearing nothing daylong but the shells and beads braided into her black hair. Here, where he is now, everything is in unison with love and nature, and all that is true, fitting, and natural in a passion is proper and legitimate. As she teaches him in her silent and voluptuous acquiescence.

How did he come to such a place? Perhaps he lost his way, or was sent by the army, or was chased by lawmen, or went in purposeful search of some secret treasure or his own self-knowledge, or perhaps he was captured and dragged to this alien land, stripped, bound, spread-eagled on the desert floor to be tortured and killed, only to be rescued at the last moment by the great chief's only daughter, straddling his condemned body with her innocent one, staying her father's hand with her tender plea as she knelt over him, dressed merely in her tinkling shells and beads, a rare sight unseen by him just so before, and one that, in spite of the extremity of his circumstances, arouses in him a most profound agitation, the evidence of it rearing up before their astounded eyes like a hostile totem erected on the arid plain—which in turn arouses in the men of the tribe a contrary emotion and, in a rage shared by all of them, a young brave, one of her brothers, or a suitor, or both, staggers forward with a tomahawk to chop down the hateful thing. To save it from destruction, or simply to hide it from view, the beautiful pagan princess impales herself upon it, screaming with the sudden pain, her coppery back arching, blood dribbling in a hot stream down over his groin. Like a baptism, he thinks, a blessing, a sweet salvation, his pinned body gratefully discharging its own boiling fluids like a surging revelation into her moist interior. No choice now. He's set free, yet unfree: one of them.

Life with the tribe, which follows as a river follows its bed, is, though always harmonious in this idyllic wilderness, not always painless. To initiate him into their exemplary ways, his new brothers play face-kicking, fire-throwing, and dodge-the-arrow games with him, rub him with skunk oil and hang him upside down in the sun without water and food for a week, cage him with rattlers, pierce his scrotum with sharpened hawk quills, chop off one of his fingers, and send him out to wrestle buck naked with a seven-foot black bear. They display their own scars and mutilations to show he isn't being picked on, it's all just for fun, part of their guileless way of life. While educating him in the art of scalping, they provide him with a wild coyote to practice on, failing to inform him that it is usually judicious—a lesson he learns almost immediately while losing a second finger—to kill the scalp's owner before trying to slip a knife in under its hairline, the consequences of his ignorance providing further entertainment for his stony-faced but attentive pagan brothers.

Everything here gives delight or else fuck it, that's the essence of their religion, as best he can understand it. The white baby, for example, adopted survivor of some massacre or other, perhaps the same one in which he himself was captured—if—is a favorite tribal toy until its colicky crying disturbs the sleep of his Indian maiden's chieftain father, whereupon he is called upon to swing the squalling thing by its feet against a tree and bash its little brains out, which is one of the easier tasks they ask him to perform. Compared, say, to the hard work of skinning buffaloes, then curing their heavy hides, stitching them into tipi covers, robes, and winding sheets for the dead, turning the bones into knives and arrowheads, hoes and dice, the fat into soaps and the tongues into hairbrushes, the paunches into water buckets, the sinew into bowstrings and tipi thread, and the scooped-out scrotums into hand rattles. All this, with typical patience and forbearance, the tribe teaches him how to do. Likewise how to slit throats, impersonate animal spirits, break mustangs bareass, wipe snot on dogs, woo his love on a magical flute with songs borrowed from the rutting bull elk, eat nits out of his own armpits.

The young Indian lass meanwhile loves him openly, freely, with a love as pure and as wholesomely naive as this land of her birth is free of the evils of the civilized world from which he's come, as evidenced by his telltale pallor and embarrassing ignorance of wigwam etiquette. She feeds him and bathes him and dresses the wounds inflicted upon him by his brothers and ornaments his naked body with horned caps and silver pendants on rawhide thongs and bear-claw necklaces and welcomes him generously into all her orifices. She cures his bellyache with skunk cabbage and wild mint, sucks out his earwax, tells his fortune. She looks into his hands and his eyes and the entrails of a dead badger and prophesies that, after many moons have passed, his old life will beckon him once more and he will abandon her and his newfound brothers and sisters and so cause her to die of a broken heart, if worse does not befall her. He does not believe this, and tells her so while beating his chest in the manner that he's been taught, yet somehow, he knows that it is true.

First, however, they must marry, something he mistakenly supposed they had already done, and in preparation for this event a special purgative ceremony is required, known as the dance of the errant bridegroom. The medicine man cuts holes in his breast on either side of his two nipples and skewers the holes with wooden pegs attached to rawhide ropes, and he's made to dance at the end of the ropes until the pegs pop out. When they don't, they hang him by the ropes to the central pole of the medicine lodge, his ankles and privy member weighted down with buffalo skulls (a form of mercy, his brothers assure him, with commiserating nods and unsmiling winks), until they do, while the older warriors prod him rhythmically with spears and arrows to the beat of a tomtom and carve religious symbols in his buttocks. Fortunately, after the

23

first peg rips out, he's told, the second follows quickly, but meanwhile the pain is such he is only conscious part of the time, drifting in and out of nightmares about the corruptions of civilization and the horrors of the cosmos as depicted by the animal kingdom and visions of the future as foretold by his bride-to-be: yes, he will leave her; the terrible pain engulfing his heart tells him so. Perhaps he will say his sad goodbyes while lying beside her in the beech woods, in which the squirrels skip, the wild deer browse, and the wistful redbird sings. Or while enjoying her from behind while she is bent over at the riverbank, laundering her father's ceremonial shirts and breechcloth, riding her horse-fashion and pulling on her braids like reins. Or perhaps he will wait until they can share one last delectable bath together. She has predicted his eventual farewell, it can come as no surprise, and yet her beautiful face seems to darken and flatten out with the shock when he tells her, her eyes to narrow, her cheekbones to rise in rage, her lips to thicken with an unspeakable fury. The next thing he knows, her powerful hands are at his throat and he is far under water, fighting for his life. He flails about desperately but cannot seem to find the rest of her, just her sharp-nailed hands closing around his windpipe and pressing him deeper and deeper—*No! Stop! (glub!) I'll (blub!) stay! I'll—*

❖ ❖ ❖

He takes a deep breath and, in the oak-framed mirror, examines his new duds: a fringed and beaded buckskin shirt with matching leggings, soft and bleached a golden hue, glossy new boots with silver spurs, the boots embossed with shootout, stampede, and campfire scenes, a white tengallon hat with silky white neckerchief, and hand-tooled gunbelt. He fills out these things in ways unfamiliar to him, as though he might have swelled up in the long soak. He's clean-shaven, barbered, and his nails have been trimmed. Pulling on a pair of snow-white kid gloves, thin as new skin, he counts his fingers: all there. His old rags are gone, nothing left of them but for his rumpled wide-brimmed hat, afloat on the soap scum in the wooden tub, and the braided scalp knotted to his new gunbelt. Whereon are also strapped a pair of engraved, silver-plated, ivory-handled Peacemakers and, in its own rawhide sheath, his old bowie knife, wiped clean and polished up so bright he can see himself in its blade, the staghorn handle newly silver-studded as though to marker its most recent history. He fingers all these things speculatively, and also the new Winchester leaning there with its hand-carved mahogany stock and engraved brass fittings, meditating the while upon his old felt hat, once dun-colored, now darker with the water it's sucked up, riding gloomily on the cold gray surface of the bathwater like a derelict river raft. Or the bloated back of something long demised.

Hlo, cowboy. It's the barroom chanteuse with the orange curls and the ruby in her cheek, propped up in the bed in a silky black nightgown with slots in it for putting her powdered ruby-tipped breasts on view. He takes in the sight, then turns away, picks up the long-barreled rifle to check its heft and balance. Good range and easy to draw a bead with but less lethal maybe up close, and up close is mostly what killing he's had to do out here on the desert. Might have to hack off a few inches. C'mon over here, darlin, and solace a poor widder woman with a sorely achin heart and a lonesome pussy sufferin from a sudden and dreadful deprivement.

Sorry, mam. I aint the condolin sort.

Well fetch yerself over and set yer dick t'dancin in the damn thing then, it aint overparticular about yer intentions.

Some other time mebbe.

Dont be so crool, kid. Caint yu see how I'm hurtin? Whut's eatin yu anyhow?

I dunno. He sighs, looks up. Her pale breasts have sagged somewhat, losing their perkiness, the nipples pointed bellyward now in a downcast humor. I thought I'd drowned.

She notices him staring and cups her breasts with both hands to aim them up at his face again. C'mere, honey, she says. C'mere'n nuzzle these a spell'n tell me all about it.

Aint nuthin t'tell. I wuz underwater. And then I wuznt.

Well well I declare, as proper folks'd say. But git over here closer. All this bereavin has stobbed my ears up so, I caint rightly hear yu away over thar.

It dont matter. He turns to study himself in the mirror, considering why it is he's been fitted out like this. He feels exceedingly powerful and yet powerfully vulnerable at the same time. Strange country. All this empty space, a body can see for miles. Yet it's impossible to shake the feeling that, whichever way he turns, he's got somebody or something just behind him.

We all know yu're purtier'n a pitcher, sweetiepie, but taint right keepin it all to yerself. C'mon. Give this good ole girl a little cuddle. Thet aint too much to ask, is it?

Sorry, mam. They's sumthin I gotta do. Caint even guess whut it is, but it's like sumthin's goin on twixt me'n them men down thar, and taint over yet.

Them men! They aint nuthin! Yu seen how they treat a lady!

Yup. Well. He opens the door, steps out on the landing, his rifle cocked. His new boots crunch grit underfoot. He bats away the cobwebs: a general murmurous gloom all about. Down below in the dark empty saloon, the furniture lies flung about in a tipped and broken scatter, decorated with playing cards, old empty bottles, poker chips, the odd ruined hat or broken-heeled boot, evidence of a livelier time past. Long past: dust on everything like a crusty shroud. Next to the busted wheel of fortune, the grand piano has fallen to its knees, grinning up at him its yellowed rictus grin, mirroring one he feels spreading in alarm across his own jaws: he backs into the room he has just left and shoves the door shut.

Well, says the voice from the bed, whut a unespected supprise. Always happy t'have visitors.

Aint nobody out thar, he says.

Must be they aint ready fer yu yet, she says, patting the black satin pillows beside her. There's a bottle and two glasses on the bedside table, and she's lit up a sweet-smelling smoke. Looks like yu got time t'kill, cowboy.

Yeah. Well. Whut other kind is they?

She smiles at that and her breasts pop to life again. Thet's a sight better. Now c'mere, handsome, and lemme instruct yu how them fancy britches come off.

This time the men are waiting for him when he comes out of the room, still retying his leggings. Before he can draw on them, they grab him and slap him up against the wall and he figures he's a dead man. But they heave him roughly onto their shoulders and parade him down the wooden stairs to the packed-out saloon, bellowing out "Weaned and Ropebroke," the hunchbacked piano player in his white shirt and yellow suspenders pounding away at the presumptive tune while the others stomp on the wooden floor and clap and bang bottles on the tables to the rhythm.

They set him down on top of a round cardtable in the middle of the room and crowd around, denying him any route to the floor or door. He could shoot his way out of here, he supposes, but it might get ugly and anyway where would he go except back out on that godforsaken desert, so for the moment he straightens up to his full height and gazes impassively down at them, hands on his hips, awaiting whatever's to come.

Yo, throw a gander at them *duds*, boys!

Whoo-eee! It's like he's lit up from his innards out!

Strikes me blind jest t'peer in his dee-rection!

There's a peculiar odor in the air, not one he's brought with him. It takes him a moment to recognize it as fresh roasted meat. His nose soaks in the rarity as the desert might a sudden shower. The men below him, he sees now, are waving gnawed bones about in the flickering lamplight, drumming on tables with them, shouting and laughing through mouthfuls of half-chewed flesh, washing it all down with tumblers of whiskey. Which seem to be on the house. Over their hairy and hatted heads, through the swinging doors, it's nighttime outside. He's not sure where the day has got to.

Here's to yu, champ! hollers a squint-eyed graybeard in a top-less straw boater, raising his glass, then downing its contents in a single swig. He concludes his toast with a full-throated belch that the others, encircling him, resoundingly echo. They bang their empty tumblers on the tables and more whiskey is passed around, fueling the mounting agitation.

Whoo! Dont he stink nice!

Like hot pussy on the hoof!

Jest lookit them silver six-shooters, willya!

And them pitcherbook boots!

Thet blade with alla studs in!

Thet signifies!

Thet buckaroo's been thar, man!

Should oughter nail a few studs on thet dick a his, too!

After whut it's been through up thar, it might be hard t'find!

Haw! It might be hard t'find but yu shore wont find it hard!

They roar with sour laughter and whistle and hoot and toss down the whiskey, pour more. Just what's so funny is not clear to him, but whatever it is he knows he's at the center of it. He would like to unpedestal himself out of their regard, but there is no gap in the bodies crowded round. He feels like a bottle set on a rock to be shot at. The spidery-fingered humpback bent over the piano has switched to "I Never Done It," a song about a gunslinger who convinces the judge that it was his gun that did the killing, not him, so the judge lets the gunman go and hangs the pistol, and all the others now join in on the chorus, snorting and whoopeeing and throwing steak bones into the air.

I never done done DONE it!

He'd be willing to take seconds on any of those throwaways but he can't say so, and none pass close enough for him to grab. But then, unexpectedly, the hunchback imitates a drumroll and tinny fanfare on his piano, an aisle opens up in the saloon mob, and a sleepy-looking halfbreed in banker's pants, red undershirt, and stovepipe hat comes down it, as though emerging from the turning wheel of fortune, ceremoniously porting a clay platter heaped up with some kind of vittles.

Here they come, boy! says a tall bald man with handlebars and a hideous scar across his face. We been keepin the sweetest grub by fer last!

The cream a the crop!

We saved em fer yu!

We reckon yu *earned* em!

Yu need t'recoup yer load back, kid!

On the clay platter lie a pair of large uncooked testicles, still bloody and pulsing like a hairy heart. It occurs to him then that what they are all feasting on is most likely his mustang. No thanks, he says. I done et.

He knows right well this faint dodge will avail him nothing, and it does not. I'm afeerd them raw prairie oysters is all yer'n, high roller, the old gent with the squinny informs him flatly, unloosing a gob that rings an unseen spittoon, and the others, closing up the gap again, chorus him with chilling insistence. Pistols have been drawn throughout the saloon.

Reluctantly, he takes up the platter being forced upon him. The grinning men cram around the table to witness this refection, licking the greasy fingers of their free hands, sucking bottles dry.

Keerful, boy! Dont grease up them new buckskins!

Aint they purty! Soft as sateen!

Soft as the schoolmarm's crupper! Aint thet right, kid? When he doesn't answer, they ask him again: Aint thet *right,* kid?

Caint say, he replies cautiously, picking up the dubious repast and sniffing it. Aint never seed the schoolmarm's crupper.

That sets them all to howling and hooting and shooting off their firearms. If he could throw them off guard somehow, he still might get out of here, but he cannot think what might now surprise them. Awright, now tuck in thar, dammit, growls the rangy scarfaced man with the gleaming dome when the ruckus dies down, pointing at the plate with the barrel of his gun, afore yu git us all riled up!

The testicles have the outward savor of gristly sponges soaked in urine with a strong whiff of the mustang's asshole clinging to them, but he holds his breath and shoves them in, all the while watching his watchers for some lapse in their red-eyed attention. If he'd had some hope of passing this ordeal quickly, that hope soon withers. The tough rubbery scrotum will not surrender to his grinding teeth and in the end, so as not to throw up, he has to swallow the bloody mess whole, a process that seems to take forever and he thinks might kill him. Certainly any notions he may have nurtured about whipping out his new six-shooters and blasting his way out of here are entirely undone by the suffocating nausea that grips him and makes his knees buckle. He closes his watering eyes to concentrate on the simple task of ingurgitation and when, the lump sliding bellyward at last, he opens them again, he finds that his gunbelt and buckskin breeches have gone missing and a passageway has opened up from the table to the grand piano. What's worse, he has been overtaken by a terrible prurience, so powerful and disturbing that that threat of hammering silver studs into his organ, so suddenly engorged now, seems less a menace than a means of relief. It feels as if it wants to burst right out of itself like a sausage puffing up on the fire.

Haw! Looks like them hoss balls done the trick!

Time fer him t'meet the marm!

The table is tipped from behind; he falls, smacking his bare nates on the tabletop, skids to the floor. At the far end of the aisle, in great distress, held down on the piano by the men of the saloon, is the pale widow woman he has seen twice before. He stumbles toward her, intent on rescuing her, or pretty sure he is, poked and prodded from behind, tugged forward by his own quivering member. She is weeping, her limbs outpinned, tossing her head from side to side, her tight dark bun coming unraveled in her anguish, her black dress twisted around her body. She cries out in alarm when she glimpses the enflamed state he's in, wrenches away, begging for mercy. Dont worry, it's awright, mam, he gasps, gripping the offending element in both fists, but he's not certain that's true. He can't even hang on to it; it keeps jumping out of his grasp with a prickly life of its own.

Thar she is, kid, snarls a scrubby little wall-eyed runt with side-whiskers. Go git it!

I caint! I—I jest had some!

No, y'aint, says the scrub, his eyes rolling in contrary directions. Not none a *this*, cowboy.

Nobody has, son. We been savin her back.

Her bodice is ripped open, her skirts flung back, exposing the webbed complications of her underclothing. And also the proximity of her flesh, the awesome profundity of it, beneath this frail wrap.

It is that wrap, that delicate black armor, that he is determined to protect, with his life if need be, even as his hands, unbidden, rip it to shreds. He clenches them into fists to bury the clawing nails and the fists punch the air wildly as though trying to escape the governance of his arms. Dont be skeered, mam, I wuz jest leavin, he wheezes, as his hips slam in between her forcibly spread thighs with the power of a bucking bull, his body's uncontrollable violence terrifying him as much as it does the agonizing woman below him.

Hell fire, whutsamatter, kid? Dont yu know whar t'stick the fuckin thing? grumbles a goateed fat man in a black string tie and gambler's broadcloth coat. Irritably, the man flicks away his cigar butt and takes hold of the bucking organ to steer it in. That does it. His flying fists have been just aching to reach out and bust something solid: in relief, he wheels now and slugs the fat man so hard in the face he drives his red pocked nose completely inside his head; he has to give a hard yank after to suck his fist out before the fat man keels over backwards, his goatee now poking up like a feather duster over the puckery soft hole between his eyes, which have come together like kissing billiard balls.

Though for a moment the blow liberates his mind and hands from their tempestuous assault, it doesn't stop his member from seeking out its target on its own. As it batters at her portal's last velutinous defense, she looks mournfully up at him and begs him to pray with her, please, before fulfilling his desperate designs, and she nods toward a Bible lying beside her on the piano top. My pleasure, mam, he gasps, his hands grabbing up the Bible as though to tear it to shreds (has he already breached her last line of defense? something soft, furry, wet—!) and inside it, buried in cutaway pages, he finds an old pistol with a black leather handle—he whips it out and blasts away at the lowlife surrounding him, starting with the drunken rubes pinning her limbs. The dead ones go down like lead sinkers and the live ones scatter as though blown out of the place by a high wind and he feels a prodigious heaving in his loins that blinds him momentarily with its explosive intensity.

When he opens his eyes again, sprawled out on the grand piano with his bare butt in the air, the saloon is empty except for the dead bodies lying around like lumpy gunnysacks and the hunchbacked piano player, sitting alone at the keyboard in his yellow suspenders with a hand-rolled cigarillo dangling from his liverish lips, knocking out a little tune which he recognizes as a taunting nursery song. Even the beautiful widow woman is gone, all evidence of his powerful emission likewise, the Bible, the black-handled pistol, the fearsome prurience. But his buckskin breeches are back, draped over a nearby chairback, along with his gunbelt and fancy new weapons, his white kid gloves with the fingertips cut away.

Whut's yer relationship to the lawr, kid? the piano player asks him around the bobbing tobacco stick as he rolls off the piano lid and goes over to haul his golden pants up and strap the belt back on. The children's song has been displaced by something more elegaic. A dirge maybe.

Aint got one. Yu the sheriff?

Nope. Jest a deppity. We're a mite short on sheriffs. Yu lookin fer work?

I dont think so, he says, but he sees he doesn't have much choice. There's a badge already pinned on his fringed shirt: a bent-tipped star pierced by a bullet hole and black with blood.

Howdy, sheriff.

Yo, sheriff, how's tricks?

The men in the street greet him affably and tip their hats as he and his deputy step out of the saloon onto the wooden sidewalk in the glazed light of midday. He touches the brim of his tengallon in reply, his other hand clutching his cocked rifle, unsure as yet of the men's true intentions. They are dragging some portly redfaced man in a crumpled top hat and three-piece suit toward a gallows that is still being knocked together in the middle of the dusty street.

Whut's happenin here? he wants to know, for he reckons it now to be his office to inquire into such civic doings.

Aw, it's jest the damn banker, sheriff. Taint fair him havin alla money and us none, so we're stringin him up. The little fat man's pockets are stuffed to overflowing with stocks and bonds and paper money, and bills stick out under his hat brim and from the tops of his boots. Paper trails him, scattering in the desert wind, as far back as the doors of the bank.

But aint yu sposed t'try a feller afore yu hang him?

Naw, sheriff! Haw!

We aint got time fer thet kinder bullpoop.

Well I aint been in this job long, but thet dont seem right.

Out in these parts it does, sheriff. It's how it's done.

Yu aint fixin t'fuck with how things are, are yu, sheriff?

I aint fixin t'nuthin. Jest aimin t'do my job proper.

The mob stands there in his way as though challenging him to give them his approval or face big trouble, their faces obscured in black shadows cast by their hat brims. He's not fearful of them, he's tempted even to have it out with the scum, but they may be right about the law, who's he to say? he's new to this line of work. Well awright, he says and clears his throat. Jest this one time, then.

He watches as, grinning their shadowy yellow grins under the fierce noonday sun, they tow the condemned banker through the dust toward the gallows. His scrawny deputy, hunched over beside him with a cigarillo between his liverlips, has remained silent through all this, and he feels uneasy, as if he might have said and done less or more than he should have. So whuddayu figger, deppity? The badge newly pinned to his buckskin shirt seems to lie right against his skin, the rimmed bullethole in it pressed round his left nipple like a hot cookie cutter. Like tying a string around a finger not to forget something and then setting it alight. Whut should we rightly be doin?

I dunno, says his deputy, pinching the cigarillo butt in his thin gnarled fingers. He hacks up a clot and arcs it a couple of yards into the water trough, then tucks the cigarillo back in his mouth. Spect we should mebbe oughter git over t'the bank.

The deputy hitches up his pants and, rocking back and forth on his short bowed legs, moseys off that way, with the sheriff tagging along behind like someone who might belong here. Well, maybe he does. Doesn't belong anywhere else, and it sure beats hauling his wretched ass all alone across that desert out there. Until now he's always been homeless as a cloud shadow, as a dying cowpoke he once met described himself while passing on, but whether by choice or luck or nature, he can't say. Just that he's always kept moving, as though moving were the same thing as breathing and giving up the one might finish off the other. Maybe that departing poke passed it on to him like an infection or a case of crabs. Though there was a time, he remembers, or seems to, when for a brief space he settled down and took up sheep ranching. He'd won twenty dollars one night in a keno game and bought the whole ranch for that, including a hundred head of sheep, a potato field, a wife, and six or seven kids, counting it a bargain, even though the rancher he bought it from, a hulking blond-bearded man with steel-blue eyes, was grinning when he took his money. He learned the sheepherding, shearing, and butchering trade, worked hard at it, and might well have lived and died a sheepman on the prairie, for it seemed like something worth doing, even if in truth he hated every minute of it. But then one day the cattlemen came and killed all his family and burned the ranch down and shot the sheep and dug up the potatoes and then pissed on everything to kill the grass and spoil the edibles, and that was the end of his twenty-dollar adventure in the granger life. He remembers staring down on that vast expanse of dead pee-soaked sheep like it was yesterday. They lay about like muggy wet clouds fallen from out the sky, as indecorously out of place in those scrubby fields as he was, and, without mentioning their unfortunate condition, he managed to trade them off to a neighbor, sight unseen, for an old broomtail hobbler, and he left that part of the country and never looked back. His memory of the family he had for that time is less substantial. All he recalls is that before they got killed they ate a lot. Some time later, he ran into the man who'd sold him the ranch, and the fellow, who'd gone off to be a lumberjack and work on the railroads, remarked over a friendly glass of whiskey that acquiring property was nothing more than laying claim to a burial plot and so put too early an end to things. Death is more fun, he said with a weary blue-eyed wink, his gun on the table, ifn yu let it sneak up on yu unawares in places where yu thought yu'd ducked it.

He and his deputy follow the trail of paper money through the sunbaked street toward the bank, and as they pass the claims office, which seems to have crossed over the street and turned halfway round since the last time he saw it, he can hear a row boiling up inside. I claim yu're a nogood snot-ugly varmint, he hears one man holler, and another shouts back: And I claim I'm gonna bust yer fuckin ass! There are gunshots and someone crashes through a plate-glass window.

Uh-oh. Reckon we oughter go see whut's goin on, deppity? he asks, sweaty kid-gloved hand on his pistol butt.

Now, dammit, sheriff, ifn yu let ever little shit thing distract yu, how we ever gonna git our job done?

His deputy seems to have lost his hump on the walk over and now has to take off his hat and duck his bald head going through the bank doors. Inside, the place is wrecked, furniture busted up and heaped about, windows measled with bullet holes, obscenities all over the adobe walls, and money is lying around everywhere. A little boy comes in behind them and picks up a coin, and the deputy whirls round and shoots him dead. Jest caint abide a thievin brat, he growls around his brown cigarillo, and he picks the boy's body up and hangs it on a coat hook. His deputy has an ugly scar, he sees now, across one eye and down into the other cheek. He might be hard to recognize but for the yellow suspenders. Y'know, when it comes t'metin out justice, sheriff, he says, the cigarillo bobbing like a wagging finger, yu'd appear a smidgen slow on the draw.

Ho, sheriff, about time yu got over here, greets the bank teller, pocketing his wire-framed spectacles and adjusting his sleeve garters. Whut with all's been goin on, I aint had no one t'spell me, and I'm sorely pinin fer a quick snort. So how about yu jest take over here at the winder a minnit whilst me'n the deppity go wet the whistle?

But I dont know nuthin about bankin.

Hell, me neither, sheriff. Fuckin mystery is whut it is.

His deputy lays a cold bony arm around his shoulder and, his breath smelling like rotten leather, whispers raspily in his ear: Watch out fer them gold nuggets in thet vault over thar, sheriff. Then he and the teller leave him, heads ducked and laughing bitterly, and he goes over to check the vault: no nuggets, nothing in there but rat turds and a few sick flies. He tries, just the same, to close the heavy steel door, but it falls off its hinges, slamming the wooden floor with a thundcrous *kerwhump*! It just misses the toes of his new boots and sends paper money fluttering into the air like chickens trying to take off, or like dead leaves stirred up by a sudden blow, a memory from some forgotten time of trees, of whole forests of them, back before he entered on the desert.

He peels off his white kid gloves to give his hands some air and then, for lack of any larger inspiration, he tucks the cigarillo in the corner of his mouth (he recalls now that the deputy, before leaving him, stuck his own half-smoked butt into his lips like a kind of advance on his wages and then, grinning a crooked grin, snapped a long bony finger at his badge, sending a sharp pain through him like a sudden toothache in the breast) and sets about sweeping the scattered money into a corner with a broom. The building, though hot and airless, has a dank underground smell that spooks him, as does that dead kid hanging there, one shoulder hitched up over his head by the hook, the other hanging limp below his gapping chin, which has been half shot away. It's so uncomfortable-looking, it makes him feel all pent up, and he regrets that this sheriffing business, which he perceives will take some getting used to, hinders him from just going off on a bust and getting wholesomely tanked and then shooting things up and stomping a lot of people until he can calm down. He recollects something a lawman once told him—or it might have been some outlaw he partnered up with for a time: Lawr'n order, son, he said, is a lot like shittin reglar: mostly makes the day run smoother, but folks need a violent dose a the trots now'n then jest not t'git all stoppered up'n lose their fightin edge.

While he's meditating on the shit side of the law and how it might play out in his new career, the barroom chanteuse with the orange curls and ruby-studded cheek comes in with four or five men masked in neckerchiefs and walks up to his grille at the counter.

Though she looks like she's probably up to no good, he tells her howdy in a sociable way and asks her if she wants to make a deposit.

No, but I'd be mighty grateful ifn *yu* would, sheriff, she says back with a wink, digging at herself between her legs with her left hand while pointing a pistol at him with her right. Actually, darlin, it's a holdup.

Well, he sighs, I should oughter arrest yu all, but they aint nuthin wuth stealin. The gold nuggets is already gone.

I know, sheriff, we stole them some while back. Whut we come fer t'day is thet silver badge yu're sportin.

No, caint let yu have thet.

Now yu aint sayin yu wanta die fer thet dang tin star!

Nope. But I aint givin it up neither.

Now aint thet feller fulla beans!

Lissen at him blowin smoke!

I think I reckanize the sumbitch, Belle, says one of her fellow desperadoes, a one-eyed graybeard with a lumpy nose, best he can tell behind the bandanna. Thet thar's the dude whut done in Big Daddy.

Yu dont say!

Hell, lets jest whup his weedy butt and take thet star, Belle!

Yeah, and all them fancy duds t'boot!

I could strictly use me a blade like thet!

Now jest git a grip on yer dicks, boys! Dont wanta mess with the sheriff when he's all hotted up like this. Yu seen whut he kin do when his dander's up. The chanteuse hitches one breast as though repocketing it in its cup and gives his golden buckskin breeches a slow affectionate study, then peers up at him and winks dreamily, scratching her crotch with her pistol barrel. Best we rob sumthin else.

Aw shit, aint all thet much here, Belle, whines a runty pop-eyed bandit with ears tattooed like spiderwebs. Most everthin's tuck whut's wuth takin.

Well, says the chanteuse languidly, and the pistol goes off between her thighs, sending a bullet ricocheting around the hollow bank lobby like a hornet on a tear—he ducks as it whines past, and it caroms hollowly off the steel doorframe of the vault, then exits through a window, where, outside in the noonday sun, a yelp is heard, though whether animal or human, hard to tell. When he raises his head, his own six-shooters drawn, he notices there's a hole in the chanteuse's skirts he can see clean through like a peephole into nothing, and there are only two or three men in here now where before there were more. She licks her smoking gun barrel suggestively, and says: They's thet boy hangin thar. I reckon we could steal him. Thet awright, sheriff honey?

The boy? He's kinder sorta dead.

I know. Little peckerwood warnt wuth cowpie when he wuz kickin, but in his present condition he's got some doobobs we can sell. Or eat.

How about it, sheriff? demands a masked fat man wearing batwing chaps and a soft tattered vest, split from armpit to hem. We gotta shoot it out or whut?

He stares through the grille at the chanteuse and her disreputable gang, weary of this exchange and wondering if maybe he ought to take up some other trade altogether, like prospecting or cattle rustling. Or maybe just throw in with the chanteuse and her warm powdered bosom; who's he to right wrongs and punish evil? His gaze is drawn into the hole in her skirts as toward a far hazed horizon which he knows to be both a promise and the absence of all promise, and so a terrible and fatal lure, and it brings to mind something else that steely-eyed sheep rancher said, or maybe it was the dying cowboy: They aint nuthin wuth dyin fer out here, pard, he said, cept choosin yer own dyin, and dyin fer it aint choosin it neither. Inbetwixt times, yu jest keep on adventurin on accounta the generalized human restlessness and cuz the end of whutall else is emptiness and the end of adventurin is emptiness too. He pulls his attention up out of the hole and out of his doleful cogitations, which have taken a spell, though no one seems to mind. Well the boy aint like proppity, he sighs, this decision having come to him, somewhat like the town did, rather than he to it. He holsters his pistols, flicks the butt away. Do whut yu damn please. And, taking up his rifle, he leaves the thieves to their drear pickings and steps out into the sudden desert night.

❧   ❧   ❧

The first thing he sees as his eyes adjust to the moonless dark is the hanged man twisting melancholically on his rope. His fancy eastern duds are gone, probably stolen; he's naked except for weathered cowhide chaps, old busted-up boots, and a round felt hat, which cozies his head down to his nose. He looks like he's chewing a dead cigar with his ghostly butt and drooling tobacco juice from it; probably a roll of paper money shoved up there and set alight in respect of some juridical tradition from these parts; his mouth's stuffed with it too, in and around the erected tongue. The creaking of the gallows rope, a distant howl, and his own footsteps in the grit of the empty street are the only sounds to be heard.

In the dim starlight, that grit glows pallidly all the way to the encircling horizon, the town's shabby structures negatively silhouetted against it, or else blackly lost in the black sky, discernible only where they blot out the stars. The hanging banker's his lone companion out here: all's shut down, even the bank, back there somewhere in the night behind him. The saloon, too, of course, no use looking in there, he knows what he'd find. He should have asked his deputy where the jail was; he could have spent the night in it. Assuming the night's his for spending in a place like this.

He sorely misses his mustang now. Though it was its locomotory aspect that he most valued on the way here, now it's his thoughts that are most afflicted by the horse's absence. Astride it, he always seemed to know where he wanted to go, what he was meant to do. It even, oddly, made him feel rooted somehow, and thus somebody, somebody with a name, even as they drifted, he

41

and the horse, uncompassed yet resolute, across this boundless desolation. The creature was a living part of him, which fit him as if born with him like his hat and boots, but it shared his miseries, too, his pains and hungers, absorbing some of them as rags might stanch a wound. And he'd got used to the view. Down here on the ground, he feels somewhat blinkered, things risen up around him that used to be mapped out below at some safer remove.

Not that he was gentle toward that evil-eyed bandy-shanked old cayuse, as he referred to it in his more sentimental humors. He respected it and shared what little he had with it, but it possessed a wayward mind of its own, and when it got too refractory, he had to take the whip to it or dig his spurs bone-deep into its flanks and haul on the bit till its mouth frothed and bled. Couldn't let the dumb beast beat him.

Though in the end it did. They'd been out under that scorching sun for what seemed like years when they struck upon a fresh watering hole: just seemed to pop up out of nowhere. The rim of it was littered with the bleached bones of men and horses and he supposed it might be poisoned so he let the horse drink first to see what would happen. Nothing did, so he joined the horse at the edge, drinking with his face in the water and then from his hat. The water was clean and sweet and so cold it made his teeth ache. He soaked himself, filled his canteen, and got ready to move on, but the horse had contrary notions and wouldn't budge from the spot. This was stupid, there was nothing to eat, no protection from the blistering sun, and anyway it made no larger sense, but the cantankerous thing seemed ready just to give it all up and toss in there with all those other anonymous bones. He talked to it, cajoled it, cursed it, kicked it, tried to lead it away on foot, yanked on its ears and bridle, used the horsewhip on it, his rifle stock, but the useless old scrag would not move; it was as still and stubborn as stone. Then, after he'd been whipping it mercilessly until his arms were ready to drop, he saw that what he was beating *was* stone and the damned horse was over on the other side of the hole, head down, still serenely lapping up water. He was furious. He whistled sharply at the perverse beast and it stepped toward him, into the water, and disappeared. In panic, he dove in after it, but the hole was only a foot deep and he hit the bottom hard. The water was warmer now and tasted salty and stung his eyes. When he could see again, he saw that the horse was standing in the same place where he'd been beating it before and the stone was gone. So he shot it. Enough was enough. On its side, the wounded animal kept quivering and kicking at the air and it had a pitiful expression on its face, so he put the rifle to its ear and finished it off. That was when, looking up from what he'd done, he first spied this town shimmering out on the horizon. He left the saddle and trappings behind on the dead horse, figuring to come back for them later, and set off walking across the desert toward the town, exhausted from his mad struggle, his legs heavy as sandbags, half dozing even as he stumbled along, regretting what he'd done of course, man always hates to lose his horse—and then one black moonless night, a night not unlike this one, there he was, slumped in the saddle, with the mustang plodding along under him like always, a dreadful thirst upon him like he'd been sucking salt, and his canteen empty.

As though provoked by his retrospections, there's a faint snort and whinny up the street. Can't see a thing in the black night, but he heads that way, pausing to cut a coil of frayed rope off the saloon hitching post. He's not at all sure what he'll find, maybe another wild horse wandered into town, even his old mustang resurrected again, but, whatever it is up there, he estimates that, if he can see it, he'll appropriate it and ride it out of here. The flat shapes crowding in on him as he passes them seem less like buildings than their absence, like black gaps in the world, and he recollects walking this way under the noonday sun and having the sensation even then of other buildings lurking like shadows behind the buildings he could see. Not that he credits such apprehensions. The usual jitters of the ingenerate gunfighter, he's familiar with such false hauntings.

Now, as he proceeds, gripping his rifle in one hand, rope in the other, he can make out a dim eery glow up ahead of him, and he recalls that it was up here somewhere that he first witnessed the beautiful widow lady, the one the men call the schoolmarm, though things may have got shifted about some on the street since last he walked it. Maybe, he thinks, maybe she's set a light out in her window, a light lit just for him, knowing he's out here and all alone and in need of some human comfort. The prospect of seeing her again spurs him on, such that soon he's broken stride and is fairly bolting along, a sudden urgency upon him and a fear of the darkness at his back—and a fear for her, too, she may be in trouble again, it's not easy for a woman like her out here, anything might be happening, and he's the sheriff now, isn't he?

He's barreling up the black street at full pelt, his head a farrago of dire yet lubricious visions, when it suddenly appears before him and paralyzes him in midstride: a majestic white stallion, more than twenty hands tall, glowing spectrally in the night from the light of the full moon, which has slid suddenly into view as if from behind a cloud in the cloudless sky. It is the most beautiful yet terrible thing he's ever seen, a powerful bluff-breasted giant of a horse, lofty in carriage, scornful of all it surveys, most particularly scornful of him, standing there in the dark street, utterly awestruck, his knees gone to jelly, his heart hammering in his ears, and he realizes that to bestride such a noble and worshipful creature was the sole reason he came out here in the first place, must have been, if in fact he did come out and was not born here. Just how he is going to capture such a wondrous beast with this miserable coil of weather-rotted rope is not clear to him, however, and when the horse snorts thunderously and rears high above him, its head haloed in its streaming milk-white mane and its mighty forelegs pawing the air as though to punch holes in the night, even that falls from his hands. Before setting its hoofs back down on earth, the great white stallion lets forth a trumpeting whinny that seems to come cascading down upon him from the very dome of the sky, echoing and resounding from all directions as though to pin him there, stunned, where he stands. As the horse snorts and paws the ground, preparing to come at him, its red eyes ablaze as if inside its cranium were a fresh-stoked furnace, he knows he can do no other than to stand his ground, exhibiting a seeming bravado, whereas in truth it's sheer terror that has petrified his limbs and nailed him to the spot. He hears the galloping hoofs before he sees the creature move, and then as suddenly it is upon him and his heart feels violently trammeled but his body remains upright and all is instantly dark and the moon is gone and the white horse, too, and he is alone once more in the vast empty night.

✧   ✧   ✧

His deputy, who is a goateed fat man with a flattened nose, finds him there in the middle of the dusty street, still rigid and locked in his boots, at high noon. Ho, sheriff, he says, picking up the dropped rope and looping it over a cocked arm and handing him his fallen rifle, we got a problem. The wimmenfolk in town is kickin up a awesome aggravation. It's jest only about gittin raped too reglar by the goddam savages, but their pants is on fire, it's a genuwine uprisin. I reckon mebbe yu better oughter talk to em.

He blinks into the blinding sunlight, lets his arms unbend and fall to his sides, the rope drop away. Talk to em? He clears his throat, spits drily into the dead air. The sign on the building in front of him tells him he's standing outside the jailhouse. I dont know nuthin about rape.

Well jest tell em it's a bad thing'n yu'll see to it it dont happen no more.

How the heck am I sposed t'do thet?

Oh, aint much to it. Them wimmen mostly only imagine all that brutified belly-bangin anyhow, they aint got nuthin better t'do, cept bake pies or warsh our underwear. So yu tell em and ifn they dont jest take yer word fer it, well we kin slap em around fer a while, or else go cut us a bonyfide scalp or two; thet should usually oughter pacify em.

He stares down at his deputy, who has eyes like little shotgun pellets buried in his lardy white cheeks and a dry unwholesome reek about him. I aint much inclined toward takin scalps.

Shore yu aint, sheriff. The deputy smirks, nodding toward the scalp hanging from his gunbelt. But we aint got no choice, do we? Ifn we let them slits git poked by a buncha wild tattooed injun buttsmashers, it might cut inta their hankerin fer civvylized dick.

Well thet aint no nevermind t'me. I'm gonna go bunk down in the jailhouse fer a stretch. This job's plumb got me bushed.

Aint no time fer thet, sheriff, here they come! He can hear them now, whooping and shrieking like savages on the warpath, sounds like hundreds of them, though there's no one in sight yet in spite of it being more or less open space from where he stands all the way to the far horizon. Them ole flytraps is really riled up, sheriff, they got a awful mad upon themselves! I reckon yu better brace yerself'n ready yer weepons, yu may hafta shoot a parcel of em!

Suddenly the main street is full of women in bright calico frocks, shawls, aprons, and sunbonnets, marching noisily seven or eight abreast, wielding brooms and rolling pins and banging tin pots, and led by the ginger-haired saloon chanteuse, the one the men call Belle, all rigged out in her dancehall costume, ruby pin in her cheek and powdered cleavage on display. He takes his deputy's sleeve-tugging advice and, cradling his rifle, steps back up on the wooden jailhouse porch for an elevated view, as the women, looking fierce and determined under the blazing sun, crowd up around below him. One of them, a tall ugly old buzzard with a frilly housecap pulled down over her tangled greasy hair, hikes her full skirts, reaches into her bloomers, and hauls out a pistol, shooting into the air. He fires and the gun flies from her hand.

Aw shit, sheriff, she yelps, squeezing her wounded hand between her legs. I wuz jest only tryin t'whoop it up a little!

Yu got a sumwhut tetchy aspect about yu t'day, sheriff hon, remarks the chanteuse with a wink, giving her breasts a hitch. Yu have a bad night?

I mighta done. Now whut's all this ruckus about, Belle?

It's them devil injuns, sheriff! They're jest at it alla time!

We caint git no peace! squawks an ancient hunchbacked granny in a hand-sewn cape and slat bonnet, stroking her beard with gnarled spidery fingers. It jest aint natcheral!

And they fuck dirty, sheriff, says an ugly wall-eyed woman dressed up in a velvet and silk wedding gown, with her fat hairy belly sticking out. Not like decent folk do.

They like t'stick it in yu all over the place, a scar-faced motherly type with a missing ear explains. Ifn y'aint got enuf holes they make some new ones! And she opens up the front of her dress to show him a few.

Now, holt on a minnit, mam—!

And lookit the dirty pitchers they drawed all over my butt! says another, raising her skirts, which look more like window curtains, to show him her hairy behind, vividly decorated with a sacred buffalo-mating effigy. It's a outrage is whut it is!

Now dammit, mam, yu jest git covered up thar!

Yu gotta do sumthin about this dreadful tribulation, sheriff! cries the chanteuse.

I'm *tryin* to!

Us proper ladies jest aint habituated t'sechlike incivil misabuse! cries the tall greasy-haired crone in the housecap. Our innercent little coosies is bein sorely afflicted!

A sweating one-eyed mestizo lady takes off her pink bonnet to fan her bald head and growls out: Show him, Belle! Show him whut them crool savages done to yu!

Well, first thing, the barroom singer says, is they hogtied me over a hitchin rail like this! She bends over the rail, her breasts spilling out, and takes hold of her ankles, while some of the other matrons tie her up there with some old frayed rope they've found in the street. They toss her black skirts up, tug her drawers down, pinch and palpate her exposed parts, and prod them with their brooms and pot handles.

Yow! howls Belle, twisting about on the rail in agony, her swaying breasts sweeping the street. This jest aint tasteful, sheriff! This aint how it oughter be!

He steps down off the porch to bring an end to this dismaying exhibit, but his deputy restrains him and the women push him back up again. Yu pay attention now, sheriff, says a squint-eyed old biddy with handlebars, burying her long warty nose in Belle's hind cheeks, but dont git too close in. This here is ladyfolk bizness.

Well jest so nobody dont git hurt here, he says uneasily, and all the women laugh at that, showing the gaps in their yellow teeth.

Dont want nobody gittin *hurt*! hoots the one-eyed mestizo lady and, stuffing a black cigar in her stubbly jowls, she rears back and gives Belle's upraised hindquarters a resounding smack with a butter paddle. The humpbacked granny follows, switching the chanteuse with a handful of wooden splints pulled out of her slat bonnet, and the others join in with whatever they have to hand from gunbelts and frypan spatulas to horsewhips, razor strops, and soup ladles, Belle screaming and yelping with each blow: Oh them dirty heathens! Jest lookit whut they done t'me, sheriff!

Some of the women now have their skirts up and are slapping at their victim's exposed behind with their own nether persons as though to parody the savages' final indignities, and Belle is groaning and grunting and sobbing something heartwrenching. A most perturbatious sight t'behold, remarks his deputy, unbuckling his gunbelt and stepping down off the porch.

Awright, awright, dammit! he yells. I git the pitcher. His deputy is already down in the hot street, half his fat bum on view, but he pulls up short and turns back, holding his pants up with both pudgy fists. So whuddayu spect me t'do about it?

We want a little lawr'n order round here, sheriff! croaks the squint-eyed old bird with the unholy nose, still whumping away bowlegged at the chanteuse's backside, her thick bloomers around her scrawny ankles, the tips of her handlebar mustache rising and falling with her movements like greased raven wings. We want justice! *Ungh!* We want some—*whoof!*—dead injuns!

All the womenfolk take up the cry for blood and justice, rattling their pans and broomsticks and firing off hidden pistols, raising a grave agitation. He figures it's about time to retire from this line of work and is fumbling with his badge when his deputy, buckling up, hollers out: Enuffa this pussywailin, yu ole scuzbags! Jest holt on t'yer britches thar'n let the sheriff'n me parlay a minnit! And he drags him into the jailhouse doorway and whispers dankly: I reckon it's high time t'call fer a posse, sheriff.

He nods, sighs. Not much choice. The badge won't come off. Snagged on something. As is he. How it is out here on the edge of things. He remembers something he once saw on a suicide's tombstone in Boot Hill, some Boot Hill: HE COME OUT HERE TO BE HIS OWN MAN BUT HE COULDNT NEVER DO NUTHIN THET WARNT NEEDFULL UNTIL HE DONE THIS AND IT WARNT NEEDFULL NEITHER. TOO BAD. RIP. He turns and, thumbs hooked in his gunbelt, faces the crowd. The womenfolk are all gone, except for the dancehall chanteuse, who is still hogtied over the hitching rail, and the street is full of men and horses.

We're rarin t'go, sheriff!

Yippee! Lets git humpin!

He would, for he's obliged, he knows, but can't. Sorry, boys, yu'll hafta go off without me, he says.

Caint do thet, sheriff. Aint a proper posse without yu.

Well too bad. Caint do nuthin about it.

Sheriff aint got a hoss, boys, his deputy explains.

No? Whutsamatter with him then?

I thought he wuz sposed t'ride the white stallion.

Thet's right, whar is thet fastuous critter? Go brang it to him, deppity.

The prospect of seeing the white stallion again, and moreover of mounting it, enlivens him and somewhat reconciles him to riding out with the scalping party. The animal looks a bit different in the sunlight, however, more like an old swayback mule in truth, though at least it's white. No tack, not even a saddle or a bridle, just a piece of rope looped around its knobbly withers. Takes him a couple of tries to get seated, and by the time he's accomplished it the posse is nothing but a puff of dust out on the far horizon. He gives the decrepit old thing a sharp spur in the flanks and they lumber off in that general direction.

Yu take keer now, sheriff hon! the chanteuse calls out from between her legs as he plods past her, her milk-white arse aglow in the noonday sun. All us righteous folk is leanin on yu!

Shore. Watch yu dont git blistered up, he says.

His old mount must have a short leg. No matter how many times he points its nose away, the town is always over there to his right like they're circling it. Or rather, like they're on the rim of some wheel and the town's the hub, for it keeps rotating with his own sluggish progress, showing him always the same distant view of the chanteuse's tiny glowing butt over the hitching rail in front of the jailhouse, nailed there like a WANTED poster. A most desolate and desolating sight, that pitiful town, clumped there on the vast empty plain like debris blown together by a passing wind, but it won't go away. Finally, having long since lost sight of the posse and weary of jerking on the rope and kicking the beast beneath him, he gives it over to a peculiarity of the landscape and continues on whatever way this sullen creature means to take him. Once, when he was still alone out on the desert (it comes back to him now, it was either before or after he shot his mustang), he came upon the skeletal ruins of an old covered wagon lying on its side, half buried in the sand. There were only a few tatters of canvas left, no cadaverous remains or abandoned chattel; it had been picked clean long ago. What was memorable about it, though, was that one of the spoked wooden wheels was still slowly turning in the dead air, round and round, as though recalling the clocking of time when there was time. He'd sat there for some time in the saddle, staring at that grinding wheel as if to stop it with his thoughts and so bring this misadventure to an end, but the longer he watched it the further he seemed to be from it, until it wasn't there anymore and he was moving along again and that town over there was shimmering on the horizon, imitating a destination.

Now, as he winds round it, he hears gunfire, hallooing, the thudding of hoofbeats up ahead, though there's nothing to be seen to account for it, whatever it is evidently obscured by a slight rise in the land which he hasn't noticed before. As they trudge up it, it seems to deflate, collapsing back to level flats once more and revealing an old wooden shack all shot to splinters, an old fellow sprawled on the ground in front of it. He pushes his sluggardly rackabones up to where the old man is lying, or maybe it goes there by itself, and he leans over and asks him if he's all right.

Shore, he groans. I been shot in sixteen places, they've cut off my arm'n et it, I got a permanent part in my hair now down t'my neckbone and a arrow up my arse, why shouldnt I be awright, yu dumb two-laigged jackass?

Oh, well, thet's awright then. I thought yu might be ailin, he says, leaning back, having captured a whiff of the old codger's reek. He appears to be the prospector type, a filthy eviscerated buckskin bag around his neck no doubt once meant for gold dust, his clothes a patchwork of old rags bound by a belt of rope, his face just a dirty beard with eyeholes in it, squinting up at him into the sun from under the turned-up brim of his soft slouched hat.

Them's purty fancy duds yu're sportin, podnuh, he says, all them thar fringes'n tassels'n porkypine quills, yu look tartier than one a them dandified joolbox coffins from out the east, which I sorely wisht I had now fer my imminent layin out in.

They aint mine. They wuz give t'me.

Do tell. A shudder ripples through his prostrate body, if it's not vermin in his clothes. And them gaudy shootin irons, he gasps when the shudder passes, kin yu use em or are they jest fer showin off?

I kin use em. Ifn I hafta.

Well yu're a sight fer sore eyes, sonny, I mean thet literal. Even hurtin as I am most elsewhars, thet bedazzlin white tengallon a yer'n plumb makes my eyes ache. Dont tell me—yu must be one a the good ole boys.

Caint rightly say. I aint one t'take sides.

The old fellow cackles drily at that and then breaks into a spasm of hollow chest-raking coughing, bouncing about on the hard ground like a Mexican jumping bean. Aw shit, he whimpers when he can and shakes his head and some sort of muck leaks out his ears. And whar'd yu git thet big white stallion, kid? Thought all them critters wuz wholly extincted. He turns his head and sends some dark spit out through the hole in his beard. Yu wanta sell it? Give yu a thousand bucks fer it.

Thet's a purty decent offer.

Hafta be on credit a course. Sumbitchin outlaw rustlers tuck everthin I got. I wuz holed up thar in my cabin in a all-day firefight standin off hunderds of em. It were mighty festive fer a time. I musta plugged fifty a them lowdown sneakthief claim-jumpin desperadoes afore I burnt up all my munitions, hadta rassle barehand with the last of em; thet's when them savages et my arm'n stuck alla these here knives in me. But ifn I'da had another gun at my side we mighta whupped them consarned butt-fuckin no-good rannahans. So whut tuck yu so long gittin here, podnuh?

I only jest got wind of it, as yu might say. He looks around at the barren plain. But whut happent to the ones yu killt?

Dunno. Aint they thar? They musta drug em off. I done em no especial favors and so they wuz purty unsightly. So how do they call yu anyways, stranger?

Nuthin. I'm jest the sheriff.

Thet figgers. They call me Goldy on accounta I aint never had none nor even seed any, wouldnt know whut the shit looked like ifn I did. Other times they call me Parson on accounta how fuckin decorous I talk, or else Mister Dude fer my smart dressin, y'know, though purty soon I spect they'll be callin me Sleepin Byooty and gittin it right fer wunst. He cackles softly again through his faceful of hair, then suddenly screws up his beady eyes and lets out with a dreadful yowl, heaving about on the ground and clutching the collar of his raggedy flannel shirt with his good arm as though to tear it away. The other arm is gone below the elbow and nothing but gnawed bone above. Oh shitfire, podnuh, this ole cuss is in a mizzerbul fuckin way! he wheezes when he's able. Damn! Y'aint got a spare chaw on yu, do yu?

Nope. Aint got no kinder provisions.

Tarnation! Yu aint good fer much, are yu, bucko? Someone fer a dyin hombre t'rattle at, thet's about it.

Aint outstandin at thet neither, ole man. In fact I gotta be moseyin along. Anythin else I kin do fer yu afore I go?

Whuddayu mean, anythin else, yu vexatious shitepoke, yu aint done nuthin yet! But awright, pard, ifn yu wanta be sociable, yu might hep me shift this ruint ole carkiss inside. I'm jest fryin up out here in thet damn sun.

Shore. He slides down off his gully-backed mount. Where he's been sitting, he notices, he's rubbed off whatever they used to whitewash the animal, and a scabious black patch is showing through. The old prospector weighs about what his rags and hair weigh; it's like picking up a dried beaver pelt or an armload of tumbleweed, his stink being the heaviest thing about him. Has to breathe through his mouth so as not to faint from it. Yu've definitely gone off, ole man, he grumbles, turning his head away.

I know it. Caint hep it. It's why they call me Sweetpea. The man has clapped his raw armbone around his neck to hold on, and it feels like he's yoked hard to something perilous and dreadful. So whut brung yu out t'this burnt-out shithole, kid? Whut set yer dumb ass on fire?

I dunno. Dont recall. Feel like I always been here.

I know whut yu mean. It's differnt out here, it aint like other places—in fact it aint a place at all, it's more like no place. Yu think yu go to it, but it comes to yu and, big as it is, gits inside yu and yu inside it, till yu and it're purty much the same thing. Aint thet sumthin! A right smarta things happen but they aint no order to em. Yu could be a thousand years older'n me, or younger, no tellin which, and it might be yestidday or tomorra or both at the same time. Y'know whut it is? I'll tell yu whut it is. It's a goddam mystery's whut. Thet how yu see it?

Mebbe. Dont meditate on it much.

Nope, spose not. Sorry about the jabber, son, it's only all whut I got left. But words aint got nuthin t'do with it, hell, I know thet, it's doin does the talkin out here in the Terrortory, it's writ in the lawr sumwhars. But alla thet doin, whar does it go? It feels like the real McCoy but it feels like nuthin, too. Like whut's in my goddam pockets ifn I still even got pockets. Oh I know why *I* come out awright, I know whut set *my* pore butt burnin. Some buggers like livin rough and humpin the natives, and others always hafta try t'make sumthin outa nuthin, but fer me it wuz the plain ole golden legend whut drug me out. I heerd tell they wuz everthin out here a body could want nor even imagine. I heerd they wuz outcroppins a gold twixt trees hanged with chains a precious jewels and rivers a the purest whuskey and fast byootiful wimmen and even the goddam fuckin fountain a youth, and, shoot, I *wanted* summa thet, who wouldnt? I wanted to be, jest like they tole it t'me, out on the adventurous stage a grand emprise. And y'know whut, son? Lean close now, I aint got much wind left.

Mebbe not, but whut yu got is terrible off-puttin.

I know, it's why they call me Baby Breath, but lissen, thet's jest whut it is, see, a stage, I finally figgered it out, a fuckin stage fer tootin yer horn on—crikey, it even looks like one—and the wuss thing is, we all know that afore we even set off. So it aint about gold at all nor land neither nor freedom—hoo! freedom, *shit!*— nor civvylizin the wilderness and smoothin the heathen encrustations from the savage mind, oh no, hell no! It's about, lissen t'me now, it's about *style*. They aint nuthin else to it. Cept fer the killin, a course, caint even have style without the killin, but thet's easy, aint nobody caint kill, it's like eatin and fartin. But dustin em with class, with a bitta spiff'n yer own wrinkle, thet's one in a million billion. Thet's the one whut leaves his name behind—his real one or his made-up one, dont matter—but thet name jest sticks like mud'n sucks everbody else up into it, and, son, yu aint gonna git nowhars out here till yu learn thet. Whut I mean t'say is, thet's mebbe a handsome sombrero yu got pushin yer ears out, but so far's I kin tell whut's under it dont amount to a pile a stale horse-poop.

Thanks, ole man, that's mighty reassurin, specially comin from a stylish gent like yerself. But I aint tryin t'git nowhars.

At the doorway, as if to prove his point, he's stopped by a skinny long-haired fellow in a black suit and bowler, a photographer by the look of the paraphernalia he's porting. Dont take the ole coot inside, he says. The light's piss in thar. I say nuthin about the smell.

He's dyin. It's his last wish. And he's hurtin bad.

Yu dont say. Well it aint gonna matter to him nor nobody else shortly enuf, replies the photographer, with a crooked gold-toothed grin, setting up his gear. Everthin passes, friend, thet's the good news. Now jest set him on this chair here so's I kin shoot his disgustin remains fer pasterity wunst he's finally kicked it.

The old prospector seems to relish the idea of having his photograph taken, even if he won't be around for the actual event, so he props him up there on the chair the photographer has dragged out of the shot-up shack. Jest lean me sideways, boys, the prospector wheezes, so's I dont hafta set on thet damn arrow.

The ole fart's gone all t'hair, the photographer grumbles from under his black hood as he peers through his lens, the greasy black strands of his own hair dangling under the cloth like spiders' legs. Looks like the ass end of a fuckin porkypine. Fit him out thar with his pick'n pan, why dont yu, make him look half human.

He does so, also loads him up with his antiquated sidearms and sets his slouch hat on square, as the photographer instructs, and then he remounts the swayback mule and prepares to move on. Whut yu need, son, the old codger calls out, is a proper sidekick. He wags his gnawed armbone at him accusingly, or maybe he's just waving goodbye. It's about the nakedest thing he's ever seen. I'da been happy t'oblige but yu come too goddam late!

I know it, he says. Dont seem to of been on time fer nuthin yet. Reckon thet must be *my* style.

That sets off another fit of cackling and wheezing and dark spewing, a sorry spectacle which he rides away from. The town meanwhile has finally sunk from sight and he is alone once more out on the vast empty desert.

It is dark, another moonless desert night, when he comes at last on the lost posse, locating them not by their campfire or bitter laughter but by the lowing of the vast herd of cattle they have gathered around them, their distant fire flickering in the herd's depths like the candlelit core of an unstable maze. They've filled up the whole prairie with the dumb shuffling beasts; he has to pick his way through thousands of them, trying to avoid their scything horns, egging on his reluctant mount, which is white now only on its underside, away from the weather; it's like moving through some viscous and muscular sea, shoving against a stubborn tide, though how he even knows about seas and tides, he has no idea. Once among them, he can see nothing else for miles around, and he worries that maybe he's fated to be rafted here above their pale humped hides forever, or anyway until his raft's old shanks give way. Gaps open between their flanks, he pushes into them, bumped and jostled from the rear, then pokes and prods with his rifle barrel to pry open new gaps, but his progress is both slow and without sensible direction, that flickering firelight itself now lost to view.

Hlo, sheriff. About fuckin time yu turned up, growls a hollow voice at his back. He bends round in his slope seat, his Winchester across his thighs. The posse's just behind him, sitting around a roaring campfire by the chuckwagon, smoking, chewing their grub, belching, drinking from mugs and bottles. A gaunt bald-pated scar-faced man, wearing his hat on his back with a cord around his throat, is blowing on an ocarina, making a low wailing noise not unlike the far-off lowing of cattle, which may be all he's heard all night, except for the sluggish thump and rustle of the chafing bodies. A one-eared mestizo with a crushed bowler and an eyepatch looks up from the old white stick he's whittling and, the light from the fire lighting up his good eye like a hot coin, asks: Whut kep yu so goddam long?

The sheriff's been out, yu know, *trail*-blazin, says another, and they all bark and hoot at that and explode a fart or two.

A wizened bespectacled hunchback in banker's pants and watch-fobbed waistcoat spits into the flames and says: Well dont be a stranger, sheriff. C'mon over'n rest yer can a spell.

He shrugs and, using his knees and raps of his rifle butt, he slowly pivots his old spindleshanks around toward the fire, but it's an obstinate creature and by the time he has managed it, cattle have crowded up around him again and the campfire seems to have receded. Between him and it: the scrawny rumps of a dozen or so cows with their tails up in the air.

Haw. Looks like yu'll hafta fuck yer way in here, sheriff, says a brawny skew-jawed lout with a bandanna headband and a thin black mustache.

Naw, them ole bossies dont fancy the sheriff, grunts the hunch-back. It's thet handsome white stallion whut's got their tails up.

Thet hoss is a real byooty awright. I feel a kinder lustful hankerin fer it myself.

Boys, I tell yu, says a squint-eyed old graybeard with a preacherly manner, t'bestride sech a hoss as thet'd be like bein born agin!

They all yea-say that campmeeting style and suck worshipfully from their whiskey bottles—Or t'*be* bestrid! Yeah! Haw! Aymen, brother!—but meanwhile the cows have nudged him further and further away until he can no longer make out the details up there: just a bunch of dark shadowy figures huddled in their hats around a cold fire, alone in the dark sea of cattle, the chuckwagon a vague glimmerous shape against the black sky like a screen hiding something.

Ho, sheriff! one of them shouts, can't tell which, his far-off holler all but lost in the shapeless prairie night. Whar yu goin? The beans is agittin cold!

Instead of cows' bumholes he's mostly looking at the front ends of steers now, their horned heads down and dangerous. In fact, he realizes that the only reason his poor old mount is still upright is that the steer that has impaled it has its horns stuck in its gut and so is holding up a creature now mainly dead. The campfire off in the distance looks no more substantial than a match being held to a cigarillo. Before it's snuffed out altogether, he cocks his rifle, shoots the steer below behind the ear, and hops off as both beasts collapse like deflating balloons. Other steers are pawing the ground menacingly but he brings them down with his rifle, then draws his six-shooters and fires away at the lot, clearing space. The sharp shocking report of gunfire in the still night causes those near him to break in panic and they charge off blindly in all directions, pounding into each other and into the massed-up crowd of those around them, spreading terror like a stone slapped into water. Soon the entire herd is on the move but with nowhere to go, the ground quavering under the thunderous buffeting of their hoofs and their colliding bodies like a bedroll being shaken out. Some of the wild-eyed creatures come running straight at him, but he holds his ground, unsteady as it is, bringing them down one by one, pumping lead into their dim cow brains, his weapons growing hot in his hands. The roar of their stampeding is deafening and more than once he is brought to his knees by the violent convulsions of the earth beneath him, but then suddenly the entire herd vanishes into the night like a slate being erased and all is still.

He holsters his pistols, picks up his fallen rifle, reloads it, and begins the long trek on foot to the campfire, stepping over and around the silhouetted carcasses that line his path back like lumpy milestones. Some of the cattle he passes are not yet dead and they gaze up at him pitiably with their big wet eyes, through which he shoots them with his rifle to make their dying short but vivid to them.

He is met at the campfire by muttering and grumbling, incomprehensible except for the swearwords, which are in the majority but add up to nothing in particular. Tell me that agin, he says.

We said yu done some serious damage to our herd, sheriff, snarls the wamper-jawed lout with the pencil-lined upper lip. In fact it aint thar no more. We're gonna hafta dock yer pay.

Thet's good news. Didnt know I wuz gittin paid.

Well it aint much. We figger after tonight's deevastation yu're about forty years in debt to us.

And thet dont include our sentymental feelins toward them pore little dogies, says the preacherly graybeard, snatching a lizard off a rock and tossing it into the fire to watch it wriggle. We been left downright bereft.

He eyes them coldly, rifle cradled in the crook of his arm. Well thet's most lamentable, he says. But whut wuz yu doin with alla them cattle anyhow? I thought yu wuz ahuntin injun scalps.

Well the problem with thet, sheriff, says the hunchback, shoving a chaw of tobacco into his grizzled cheeks, is we're plumb outa savages. Aint seed a live one with his skin still on in a coon's age. He spits into the fire to set it sizzling.

But whut about alla them misabused wimmenfolk?

All them whut?

Oh right, snorts the mestizo, glancing up with his good eye from his whittling. Hah! The wimmenfolk!

They heehaw and whistle at that and, while the ocarina player blows a dancehall tune, a pig-eyed fat man with a waxed handlebar mustache rises from his squat for a moment to drop his pants and wriggle his arse at the fire.

Well lets see, says the squint-eyed old fellow with the high manner. I estimate we did mebbe go dig up a ole burial ground fer some deceased scalps. Jest not t'disappoint, y'know. They're in a saddlebag over thar. They got a unseemly odor about em, but hep yerself.

But thet aint the point. Yu all been deppitized.

Well we undeppitized ourselves, sheriff. It jest warnt no fun. We tuck up cowpunchin instead.

Beats scalp huntin all t'blazes.

Yu eat better too, says the fat man, rebuttoning his breeches. Less yu got some trigger-happy damfool comin along'n drivin off yer larder. The others rumble and growl at that, while the fat man relights a stubby black cigar butt in the fire.

Whut I caint quite figger is whar'd yu git em all?

Git em?

Yer stock.

Well we, uh, we borried em, explains a weedy wall-eyed runt, picking his teeth with a sliver of bone.

Yu mean yu rustled alla them cattle?

Well yu dont hafta put a name to it, sheriff. But how else yu gonna git yu a steer out in these parts?

We jest kinder pass em around out here, y'see, says the hunchback, peering up at him over his wire-rimmed spectacles, his cheek bulging with chaw. He lets fly another load into the fire. It's how we do it.

I dunno. I aint never read the lawr but I think yu broke it, he says. They all just smile back blankly at him. Naw. Haw!

Whut's agin the lawr, sheriff, says the fat man around his cigar stub, is shootin up other folks' cows and runnin their herds off. Thet thar's a capital offense throughout the whole goddam Terrortory. Reckon we may have no choice but t'string yu up fer thet one. Jest t'be proper, y'know.

Less a course yu hightail it out thar'n brang em all back agin.

How'm I gonna do thet? They went off ever which way.

Shit, I dunno, sheriff. It's yer fuckin neck, yu figger it out.

I kin see thet rapscallion aint gonna rectify his heinous misdeeds.

Nor even repent of em. He's a hard case.

Only trouble is, whar kin we hang him? They aint no trees out here.

We kin use the chuckwagon, says the fat man, taking up a coil of rope and cutting off a length with a butcher knife. Ifn it aint high enuf, we'll hitch up the hosses'n drug him along behind it.

Hole up thar, buttbrain, says the one-eared mestizo with the eyepatch, rising to his feet. Aint nobody messin with the sheriff, not while I'm deppity.

Yeah? And whut yu gonna do about it, yu scumsuckin greaser?

I'll show yu whut I'm gonna do, yu mizzerbul dumsquizzled lardass, snarls the mestizo, throwing away his white stick and hurling himself at the fat man with his whittling knife. The fat man is caught off guard and the knife rips into his groin, the cigar butt popping from his lips as though triggered out by the invading blade, but he manages to plunge his own butcher knife deep into the mestizo's belly, both men grunting and staggering back before lunging at each other again.

Hey! Jest wait up thar, fellers! he shouts, raising his rifle. Stop thet!

Now dont go botherin inta other folks' bizness, sheriff, says the old fellow with the squinny, batting his rifle away. This aint none a yer concern.

But—!

Others grab him and pin his arms back. It's outside yer fuckin jurisdiction, sheriff, they grunt, raising him off the ground and roping his ankles together.

Defense is not a significant part of either man's technique. They just go at it freestyle, cutting each other over and over; it's more a matter of pace and persistence than artfulness as their bloodied knives, catching the light from the campfire, flash in and out of each other's bodies. His deputy loses his other ear and his voice pipe, no doubt more within besides; the fat man's smile is widened from ear to ear, his stiffened handlebars snicked to a brush, and his belly's so punctured his guts start to spill out; but neither man gives an inch. *Whuck, whuck, whuck*, the knives go, and nothing he can do but watch, both men blinded now by blood and injury, taking blow after blow after blow, the other men of the posse cheering them on, laying bets on the side, pushing the antagonists back into it if they chance to stagger apart. Finally, the butcher knife breaks off in the mestizo's ribs and, as the disarmed fat man slumps to his knees, the mestizo finishes him off in the slaughterhouse manner by stabbing him two-fisted in the back of the neck.

His minced-up deputy stands there, weaving about, still wearing his crushed bowler and the broken blade in his chest, his body sliced open in a hundred places and showing its inner regions, but with his own bloody knife outthrust as though ready as ever to take on all comers. The fire shimmers patchily on his chopped-up face and casts a hulking shadow on the chuckwagon behind him.

Awright, awright, deppity, we take yer point, says the brawny lout irritably. But whut about our goddam cattle?

63

The deputy, his vocal cords cut and dangling from the hole in his throat, cannot reply, but he turns to the bald ocarina player and gestures with his knife.

Reckon he wants yu t'pipe us a tune on yer sweet patayta, says the bespectacled hunchback.

The man cups the instrument in his large bony hands, bends his gleaming dome toward the fire, and once again imitates the moan of lowing cattle. Almost instantly, about as fast as the fluttered shuffle of a deck of cards, the prairie fills up all around with grazing cattle again.

With that, they set him down again and unbind his ankles. He picks up the fallen Winchester. Ifn yu could do thet, he grumps, why'd yu make sech a fuss?

Aw, sheriff, dont mind us, says the preacherly fellow with a squinnied wink, as they drag the ruined fat man away into the dark beyond the fire. We're jest skylarkin, y'know, a little cockeyed fun like cowpokes always do, it's in our nature. Now why dont yu set down'n hep yerself t'some beans'n buffalo hump.

Aint hungry. He's starved, more like, but their vittles do not appear to be of the edible variety. Wouldnt say no t'summa that whuskey though.

Haw. A silence descends as though fallen from the star-pocked sky. Bet yu wouldnt.

No one moves. Hard to read their expressions. The fire has died down to coals, painting their faces a deep crimson. Mostly, behind their thick red masks, they seem to be grinning or staring at him blankly. Waiting to see what he'll do. No choice about that. If he wants anything he'll have to help himself, and he's already manifested his wants. There's a lone bottle standing on a stone just on the other side of the fire, catching its light. Like a taunt. He watches their hands. There's nothing to be heard in the tense motionless silence but the hushed pop and crackle of the dying fire. Even the cattle seem to have paused in their grazing. He has about decided to shoot the bottle, just blast it away and ask for another, see what happens, but then his deputy leans over to pick it up, squirting jets of blood out of his wounds, and staggers over to him with it, stumbling right through the firecoals. As he hands it to him, his good eye rolls up into the back of his head and he collapses at his feet. The deathly stillness maintains. He wipes the blood off the neck of the bottle. Thanks, deppity, much obliged, he says flatly and, watching them all warily, puts the bottle to his lips.

❖   ❖   ❖

The bottle is empty. He tosses it away, listens to it clatter over the parched earth, a thin paltry sound that makes his eyes ache. He's all alone, lying on his back with his hat over his face to shield him from the blazing midday desert sun. He can see, peering out into all that light from under his hat brim, that the men of his posse, what was once his posse, have cleared out and taken their herd with them, nothing left of them but for a few bleached bones and a charred place where the campfire was. Plus a saddlebag. He doesn't want to know what's in it. He struggles painfully to his feet, trying not to fall over again; his head weighs a ton, hard to keep it on his shoulders. Near him, half buried in the sand: the skull of a steer gazing up at him with empty sockets, a note stabbed onto one of its horns. *We're over yonder,* it says. *Come find us ifn yu've a mind to. Any extry hand welcum. Yer pals the x-posse.* There's a P.S. on the other side: *Watch out fer thet rattler residin in the skull, it's a real mean fucker.* Too late. Its fangs are already driven deep into his inner thigh, its flat glassy-eyed head as big as an old scuffed boot lodged there in his crotch, its huge striped body wriggling wildly between his legs like a freak dick from a carnival sideshow.

The dull ache in his head is immediately replaced by a sharp ferocious pain throughout his lower parts. His chaps and buckskins should have protected him, but the big snake has struck in the soft part of his thigh, and now its fangs are helplessly locked there in flesh and leather. He whips his old staghorn-handled bowie knife from its sheath and cuts the rattlesnake's head off at the throat. The headless body twists and thrashes on the ground, but the severed head, even after he stabs it between the eyes, continues to gaze up at him from between his legs with a look commingled of regret, familiarity, and grinning defiance. He rips it out and tosses it away but the fangs remain like steel needles driven to the bone.

He unknots the chaps and tears at his buckskin breeches, but they're a tight fit; he can get them down off his butt but not past the snakebite on his thigh: they're like a second skin. Already his thigh and groin are swelling up and changing color and he's starting to feel sick. He knows he should suck the poison out but the bite's in a place he can't reach, even if he could get his pants down. So he cuts into the punctures through the pantleg with his bowie knife and squeezes the blood and pus out as best he can, feeling his whole body begin to puff up and turn feverish.

He figures he's done for, but then he spies the town over on the horizon, shimmering in the heat. It's his only chance. He tosses his gunbelt over his shoulder and, in a cold sweat, staggers off in that direction, stumbling, falling, picking himself up and carrying on. The poison's getting to him. Sometimes the town is out there, sometimes it isn't. He sees a soft quilted bunk that fades into sagebrush when he reaches it, a watering hole which turns into a dry gully when he falls into it, mouth open, face in the sand.

Lying there, grit in his teeth, he seems to recollect—it's sort of a memory and it sort of happens—accompanying a wagon train of emigrants heading west across the dusty plains. He might have been a hired gun or a scout or he might himself be one of the pioneers, it's not clear, but their passage takes them through endless black acres of burnt-out prairie grass, dust churned up by the wooden wheels so thick wet bandannas tied over their faces cannot filter it out (he can taste it, coating his tongue, clogging his throat), the teams of oxen plodding through it all, their hickory yokes squeaking, chains rattling, and there's the tinkling clatter of tinware, the shriek of ungreased axles, the squalling of children; he can hear all this. Storms suddenly rise up out of nowhere and sweep wrathfully down upon them, lightning bolts slamming the ground around them like electrical cannonballs, and then as quickly they sweep away again, leaving the land as hot and dusty as if no rain had passed.

In the calm after one such storm, just as they are crawling out from under the oiled canvases of their wagons, they are attacked by a band of screaming wild Indians on horseback, emerging as though out of the vanishing storm itself, their naked bodies striped head to toe with red and black paint, their long ebon hair floating to the wind, bald eagles' feathers on their heads and strips of flayed antelope skin and white feathery skunks' tails strung to their knees and elbows—they make a sight to see, though looking can get a person turned into a human pincushion. Already the settlers are falling—men, women, and children, their horses and oxen, too—with arrows through their throats, chests, and eyeballs. He seems to recognize them all but doesn't know them, except for that beautiful widow woman in black, the schoolmarm from the town up ahead, moving among the fallen, treating their injuries, consoling the dying, keeping wounded and orphaned children distracted by teaching them their ABCs.

He's having a hard time thinking, he hurts so badly and feels so sick, but he manages somehow, hitching about on his one good leg, wincing with pain and nausea, to get all the covered wagons snaked round in a circle, tongues chained to rear axles, as a makeshift breastwork against the incessant hail of deadly arrows. The clumsy wagons teeter and tip and Dutch ovens, rocking chairs, and butter churns spill out like peace offerings, plows, skillets, chamber pots, and bucksaws, a proliferation of translated merchandise that dizzies him, or perhaps exemplifies the dizziness that besets him. He and the remaining settlers knuckle down— he hears cavalry trumpets in the distance but they are stifled mid-toot, hope lost, they're strictly on their own here—to the business of killing savages, which they accomplish in great numbers; popping them off their ponies is like swatting flies, but they keep coming at full gallop in wave after wave, blowing war whistles made of the bones of eagles' wings and whooping and hollering like a troop of demons, all the while showering arrows on them so thick and fast the day turns dark, until soon there are no settlers left but himself, and he's got an arrow piercing his inner thigh, a poisoned one by the swelling sensation of it, and his mouth is full of sand.

He figures he's done for, a feeling he might have had before, but then the schoolmarm passes, scowling down at him where he lies as though offended by what she sees. I'm sorry, mam, he says, or thinks he says, it's all fading away. He knows he must be all swollen up and ugly looking down where the arrow's sticking out, and he's not sure his pants are all the way on. No matter. She produces a pair of scissors and cuts them away entirely, rips out the barbed arrow shaft like yanking a weed, then strips off one of her black stockings and ligatures his naked thigh with it, providing him just the briefest glimpse of a tender bare calf under her dark skirts, which makes him feel like crying, or maybe the pain does. She digs and snips at his wound with the scissors, then stoops to suck the venom out. The arrows are still whizzing overhead but they seem to be rising higher and higher until they are all but out of view, up where the hawks hover. He can hear her sucking and spitting, can see the tight dark bun of her hair bobbing between his thighs, but he cannot feel her lips on him, everything's gone dead below the ligature. Not above it, though. Where her hand is. When she's done, she cleans the wound with some warm liquid she's produced from somewhere, salts it with a white powder the color of potash, and pours something like diluted ammonia down his gullet, making him gag. While he's still spluttering, she shoves a long dull needle in so tender a place just above the wound that he cries out like one of those shrieking savages who have just passed by, injecting him with something from a bottle marked with a skull and crossbones. Hush now, she says, and she unties the ligature to use the stocking as a bandage, often brushing as she works the thing standing nearby, the only thing standing in fact for miles around. Before rising and leaving him there, she gazes at it sorrowfully for a moment, as if it's about the saddest thing she's ever seen.

Sorry, mam. Caint hep thet. But I'm mighty obliged. She frowns down upon him, her thin unpainted lips pressed together. There is a tiny black beauty spot on her cheek, set there, it would seem, though it's probably but a mole, to complement her long black dress. Fer whut yu done fer my laig, I mean.

Did, she says sternly. I am obliged for what yu *did* for my leg.

Yes'm. He closes his eyes. Yu're welcum.

When he opens them again, he finds himself stretched out in black satin and for a moment he thinks he's in a coffin. No, no, I aint dead! he gasps, trying to rise.

Shore yu aint, sheriff honey. The saloon chanteuse is sitting at her dressing table powdering her breasts. He falls back into the bed, feeling like he's been kicked below by a horse. Beyond the open windows where lace curtains hang limply in the midday heat, he can hear creaking wagon wheels, the blacksmith's hammer, booted feet treading wooden sidewalks, curses, whinnies, shouts, the occasional gunshot. These sounds seem aimed at him, of no more duration than his need of them, and maybe, in the way that towns talk to sheriffs, they are. Though it wuz tetch'n go fer a time, sweetie.

I wuz havin a fearsome dream. Ifn it wuz a dream. Seemed so real.

Looked purty arousin from whut I could see.

I wuz layin out on the desert. Dyin. All alone. And some wolves come by. Whole pack of em.

Dont tell me. They et yu up.

I thought they wuz gonna. And I couldnt do nuthin about it. But they didnt. They jest sniffed at me and then they all lined up thar'n sucked whar I wuz hurt and lapped at my, y'know, my manly part, like cows at a salt licks. I wuz afeered ifn I moved they'd bite it off so I hadta lay stone still.

Whenever sumthin like thet happens t'me, I git itchy all over and hafta sneeze sumthin awful.

Thet werent exactly my problem.

No, but not unlike. She winks at him in the mirror, hefts her breasts one at a time, rouges the tips. Well anyhow, thet explains how I found yu, all swoll up and ravin like yer brain wuz cracked, buckskins cut t'ribbons and peed on by some filthy animule, musta been them wolves. Yu wuz a real morbid spectacle, dearie; the whole town lined up t'witness yu when I brung yu in.

I dont member none a thet.

Course yu dont. Yu wuz stock outa yer haidbone. But outa yer pants too and cuter'n a chipmunk. I shooed the buzzards off and throwed yer dazzlin carkiss over the rump of my hoss and brung yu right down main street; we done a whole parade, flags flyin, fireworks, brass band'n all, it wuz more fun than a injun roast. Whut wuz most byootyful, though, wuz when yu ast me t'marry yu.

When I *whut*—?

Course, bein so recently widdered, I hadta think about it fer a minnit or two—

Belle! We aint hitched—?!

Well not yet, darlin, but the preacher's due here any second. I bought myself some special underbritches fer the occasion yu're jest gonna love. I'd show em to yu, but it's bad luck t'see yer bride's—

But, Belle, I caint do thet! It—it—whut kin I say?—it dont go with the job!

Fiddlesticks. I'll git yu a new job. Yu kin play the pianner.

I dont know how t'play the pianner.

I'll larn yu.

I dont wanta be larnt. She brings her ruby-tipped breasts over for him to kiss. He turns his head away. Belle, dammit, this aint right, I jest aint the settlin-down kind.

Yu'll git used to it, lovey. Anyways it's too late, yu done promised.

But yu said yerself I wuznt right in the haid.

Dont matter none, promise is a promise. Breakin one mebbe aint a capital offense around here, but the punishment fer it aint a purty thing t'watch. She leans over him and tickles his ear with one of her painted nipples. Now c'mon, handsome, give em a little smack. From now on, they're all yer'n. Or mostly all yer'n.

There's a rap at the door. It's open! shouts Belle, still bent over him with a pap in his ear, and in comes a lanky bald man with a goatee, one eye sewed shut by an ugly scar, a monocle in the other, bowler and Bible clasped at his crotch, and his collar turned backwards. Howdy do, dear friends, he says. I'm here t'hack up the connubial rites.

We're nearly almost ready, revrend, soon's I've smeared on my fixins.

Other townsfolk crowd in through the doorway. Hey, Belle! We decked it all out like yu ast! It's lookin wondrous conjugular down thar!

Thanks, boys! They's heaps a vittles, and the drinks're on me'n the sheriff t'day! I need a pair a yu t'hep me git my dearly betrothed down thar as he aint too ambulatory, but the resta yu kin go down and git started!

Yippee! they shout, throwing their hats in the air and clattering back down the stairs, the preacher whooping right along with them.

A squint-eyed old fellow with a foot-long beard and a pegleg stays behind with a thinly mustachioed rustic in a crumpled tophat, and while Belle goes back to her dressing table to pin the ruby in her cheek, they come over to haul him out of the bed.

Now wait up, fellers, I think we should probly oughter hole off jest a bit, he says. I caint even stand proper yet.

Thet's jest cuz yu're nervous, sheriff, says the top-hatted oaf as they drag him out from under the quilts and coverlets. The fellow has one arm in a sling or else not there at all, and his thread of a mustache, he sees, is branded on. Everbody's nervous on his weddin day.

Belle, I know yu're wantin t'git right at it, says the pegleg, but shouldnt he have some pants on? Anyhow leastways fer the cerymonies? He's desprit unsightly down thar, it kinder turns my stomach.

I aint finished patchin em up, says the chanteuse, wiggling her hips into a velvet and silk wedding gown. And they stink purty bad. He'll hafta go like he is.

Well aint yu at least got a ole skirt or sumthin t'hide him in?

I aint wearin no skirt, he says flatly.

And I aint marryin no cowboy in one neither, says Belle, buttoning up.

Awright, gimme it then, he says. I'll wear it.

How about yer ole pink bloomers, Belle? Them ole-fashion long-laigged ones with the gap in the back?

Shore. Dont know ifn they're clean or not, but they're backa the dressin screen. They dump him back on the bed and the old-timer clumps over there, his pegleg hammering the wooden floor as if trying to split the boards.

The one-armed yokel goes to help Belle with her buttons, so he pulls himself to the edge of the bed, intending to throw himself off. Can't crawl very far, sore as he is, but he figures he just might make it to the open window and take his chances out it.

He figures wrong. Whoa thar, sheriff, says the lout with the branded lip, and he strolls back casually and with his single arm flips him over and ropes his wrists behind his back all in one easy motion. No need t'git all ramparageous. Tyin the knot aint the end a the world.

The old graybeard comes thumping back, and though he twists and kicks and bucks, they succeed in fitting him out in Belle's glossy drawers, tight as they are on him, the old fellow holding him down while the younger one ties up the little ribbons at the knees into bows. Haw! Aint he cute!

Yu got them things on him fore t'aft, deppity, remarks the chanteuse, flouncing the ruffles on her gown. His bizness is hangin out.

They wouldnt go on tother way, Belle. We'da hadta shove his doodads up inside him. But it's awright. Saves time later on.

Yu my deppity? he asks the peglegged oldtimer.

Shore, sheriff, he says, buckling the gunbelt around his middle, while the other fellow works his boots on him. Dont yu reckanize me?

He had a rough time out thar on the desert.

Musta done.

Okay, port him on down, boys, I'm ready'n rarin!

Wait a minnit! Ifn yu're my deppity, I got a order t'give yu—

Later, sheriff, grimaces the old man, tobacco juice leaking down his beard like a muddy creek, and they plant his white hat on him and lift him by his armpits off the bed and on out the door. Right now the party's bilin up'n I'm dry as a dry desert bone.

As they drag him out onto the landing, they are met with a jubilant roar from the wedding guests below, followed by a piano roll, bottle banging, and shouted commentary, punctuated by loud whistling, on his marriage costume. His deputy reaches up and doffs his hat for him. The saloon is decorated entirely in white with pale streamers made from bleached rags and catalog paper looping from beam to beam, gauzy muslin festoons over the windows, bar, and swinging doors, white paper flowers on all the gambling tables, an ejaculatory scatter of white poker chips, and, hanging from the streamers, beams, and festoons, hundreds upon hundreds of tinkling white sticks, which he discovers upon being bumped by a few on his way down the stairs to be bones, whittled into the shapes of people and animals, mostly in copulating postures. Even the spittoons have been whitewashed for the occasion. Over behind the snow-white grand piano, leg and arm bones have been log-cabined into an arch around the big wheel of fortune, turning it into a kind of wedding altar, with the pooltable ROUND BALLS AND STRAIGHT CUES! sign tacked up inside and finer bones carved to resemble privy body parts dangling like a fringe from the top of the arch.

His presumed bride, her breasts on view and looking radiant, is passing among her guests, collecting hugs and kisses, compliments, bottom slaps and pinches, shots of whiskey, and well-wishes of the generally suggestive sort, as well as pouches of gold dust, which she stuffs down her bosom. Wedding gifts, he assumes, or else winnings from a bet, no doubt the one he's lost, a remark he makes to his deputy, who says: Naw, sheriff. Haw. It's fer yer weddin night. She's chargin admission.

They aint gonna be nuthin t'see, he grumps, and the deputy laughs at that, showing the gaps in his tobacco-stained teeth.

She did tell us it might be sumthin of a skin game, he says.

This un's fer yu, darlin! calls out the chanteuse, perching herself knees-up on the piano, whereupon the piano player, an earless pipe-smoking mestizo in white pajamas, strikes up a tune, and she sings him a love song about busting an unbustable bronc, the men who have hoisted him down here holding him up in front of the exuberant assembly in his buckskin shirt and gaping pink bloomers like an illustration. Not of an unbustable bronc—he's shriveled up with pain and chagrin, his wrists are still bound, his legs leaden and useless, his heart's in his boots—but of the unsavory consequences of excess civilizing. After that excitement, the preacher sets his bowler on his bald head, bangs his Bible on the bar, and calls them all forward to the tall wheel of fortune: Brang some chairs and take yer seats, gents! The blessed cerymonies is about t'commensurate!

Chairs and tables scrape on the wooden floor. The pajama'd mestizo, puffing away on his cob pipe, bangs out a kind of march tune which sounds like a horse race or else a runaway train, while he's dragged up to be stood alongside Belle. Hlo, handsome, she whispers and tweaks his more exposed features. There's a preparatory chorus throughout the saloon of throat-clearing and spitting, belching, farting, and what's either praying or cursing, and then the preacher hawks up a glomeration that rings a whitewashed spittoon a few yards away and announces: Hiyo, dear brothers and sister, we are foregathered here in most dreadful and holy joy t'harness up the sheriff to our beloved Belle, and so set him in the softest saddle in the whole damn Terrortory as I'm shore yu'll all concur!

The men shout and cheer and stamp their feet—Aymen t'thet, parson! Praise be!—and the chanteuse blushes and smiles coyly at them over her shoulder. Then she takes his near hand and claps it to her hip and says, I do! I do!

Hole on, sugarbun, says the preacher, lowering his monocle. We aint t'thet part a the proceedins yet.

Well hurry it up, revrend, she cries. I'm jest gushin out all over! And she wheels round to plant a kiss on him, throwing one leg over his bloomered hipbone and rubbing herself there, setting off a burst of hooting and whistling and the wild smashing of bottles against the white-sheeted walls.

His bad leg buckles under her weight, and the top-hatted bumpkin, holding him up with his one arm, grunts: Brace up yer carkiss, sheriff! Show a little brass'n grit thar, like whut yu're famous fer.

I aint famous fer nuthin, he gasps as the parson pulls the chanteuse off him and helps her smooth her skirts out. Cept locatin trouble mebbe.

Haw. Yu're a card, sheriff, says his deputy, spitting voluminously on the floor and stomping it with his pegleg as though it were something alive. I think yu musta overdid it at yer stag party.

Whut stag party?

Yer stag party. Y'know, on accounta gittin spliced.

But I aint had no stag party.

Wait a minnit, says the other fellow. Yu aint had no stag party?

Whut's this? asks the parson, adjusting the monocle in his eye.

The sheriff, says the deputy. He aint had no stag party!

This causes a general consternation and the chanteuse, looking a bit desperate, says: It dont matter! He kin have one tomorra! He kin have a whole dang slew of em!

Now Belle, he caint git married without a stag party, says his deputy. Them's the rules.

Aw shit, says Belle glumly, and she kicks over a white spittoon with such vehemence she sets all the little bones in the place to rattling.

Whuddayu figger, revrend? asks the oldtimer.

I figger we aint got no choice, we gotta stick to the book. But we caint conduct it here, it's too gaudied up fer sech ornery and ribald carryins on. I reckon we'd best appropriate some potables and hike him over t'the stables. Caint hurt nuthin thar and thet ole sow might still be rootin around sumwhars, firsts ifn we find her.

The men gather up armloads of bottles from the bar and what's left of the wedding banquet and, lifting him up on their shoulders, they carry him through the clinking bones toward the swinging doors, while the chanteuse hitches up her wedding gown and stamps furiously back up the stairs toward her room, unleashing a stream of violent imprecations down upon them all.

Hey wait up, Belle! Whut about our gold dust?

I'm givin yu sumbitches a rain check, she snaps back.

But it aint rainin.

Hell it aint.

❧ ❧ ❧

Shit, says one of the men, I wisht sumbody'da tole me thet ole sow wuz dead fore I poked her.

Whut differnce would it a made?

Well fer one thing I wouldna tried t'kiss her.

The men whoof and grunt sourly at that. Reckon I'm gonna hafta have a go at them bloomers, one of them says ominously. Not for the first time. He knows he has to think fast. Hard to think at all, though, nearly knocked his head off coming in here. It was pitch dark and he was mounted on their shoulders and he didn't see the top of the stable doors coming. Laid him out for a time. Now, his wrists still roped behind him, he's been sat in a feeding trough and buckled to the upright with his own hand-tooled gunbelt. They've been by from time to time to pour cheap whiskey in him and on him and smear him with horseshit and make wedding-night wisecracks, he being the particular guest of honor at this function, but mostly the men of the stag party have been downing the food and liquor themselves, sitting slumped around a kerosene lamp in an empty stall, ragging and joking and talking dirty and swatting at the horseflies and dreaming up grim escapades, often as not involving the bridegroom's physical person. Which is not in prime condition. His head is pounding, his leg still hurts from his shoulder down from whatever it was happened to him before he ended up in the chanteuse's wedding drama, and most of the rest of him has been seriously maltreated as well.

Although he is a man of few spoken words or opinions, his head is ever full of troubled thoughts, and, in spite of the blow it took, it has not lost any of them. He is a drifter and one whose history escapes him even as he experiences it, and yet to drift is to adventure and to overstudy one's history is to be ruled by it, and he is above all a free man, intent on pursuing his own meaning even if there is none. Or thus he always thought of himself before he forsook his rambling to try his hand here at the sheriff's life, and though he cannot think now why he did so, he believes it may have had to do with the oppression of loneliness which often attaches itself to freedom like a sickening and also with the presence here of the village schoolmarm, who is a mystery to him and a provocation, as she is to the men huddled around the kerosene lamp, judging by their lurid fantasies about her, now at the center of their conversation. Perhaps, too, it had to do with vanity, a desire for the esteem of others less ephemeral than that won in passing encounters with a gun or his fists. Well, he should be who he is, what trouble he's in he's brought on himself by not being so; when he's got through this misery he should, forgetful as he is, remember that and live by it as best he can, or at least such is his resolution, tied up and stinking there in the horse trough. Sorting it all out has cleared his head somewhat, which, he thinks, is probably why they thought up stag parties in the first place.

There are a couple of horses down at the far end; he can hear them snorting softly and pawing around. Though he is still crammed into Belle's skin-tight bloomers, he is also wearing his boots and silver spurs, which, through hard use, his or somebody's, have been worn to knifelike circles of steel, and it occurs to him he might be able to cut his bonds with them, borrow one of those horses, and ride out of here, if he can just get his good leg under him in the feeding trough. This is not easy, the bad leg mostly getting in the way, and consequently there's a lot of bumping and banging of steel, bone, and wood, but the men are too drunk and talking too loud about the marm to take much notice. Getting his leg under him is not the only problem. Once it's there, he recognizes, almost immediately, that it is easier to cut his butt than the ropes. Slowly, though, as he saws back and forth on the spur, he can feel them beginning to fray.

Whut really gits me, says one of the men, is her eyes. Blue and liquid as a violet's in the dewy morn, y'know whut I mean? And oh shit, her hair. It's like sunbeams twisted inta wavin golden curls, the gold I aint never struck out here. I'd like t'fuck thet hair.

Whuddayu talkin about, yu ole galoot? She aint a blonde. And her eyes aint blue, they're more like a kinder gray, the color a rain, pale'n clear like yu kin see clean through em. I'd like t'fuck them eyes.

They're whutever fuckin color I want em to be, yu wet bag a ratshit. Shet yer lip fore I dissect yer innards and make sausages outa em fer my dawg's breakfast.

Yu'n whut other regimunt, buttwipe?

Hole on, fellers, yu're both wrong, says another; they're green.

He continues to saw at the ropes binding his wrists, his attention narrowed now to this single task, but they seem almost to be growing back where he's cut them, only thicker, as if accumulating scar tissue. Her eyes is green like a medder in springtime with flecks a wildflower colors in em and bright like they's a light inside shinin out, the two of em set in a face whose pale complexion is a most genteel and suptile blend a the lily'n the rose, ifn yu ever seen sech things. And right square in the middle of it all, a perky little nose stickin straight out at yu so delicate and esposed as t'make yer heart weep fer the innercent purity of the sweet angel whut sports it. I'd like t'fuck thet nose.

Course she aint sweet alla time.

No, yu're right thar, her disposition aint always the easiest t'git on with.

Mosta the time, in fact, sweet aint the word at all.

And ifn it *aint* the word, mister, yu better go fer cover, cuz fore yu know it she'll unleash her upbringin on yu.

The marm is a formidable unleasher of upbringins.

Yu aint jest talkin jackshit, podnuh. Wunst I said *aint* in fronta her and she got me down and warshed my mouth out with lye soap. Thought I'd die a the foamin wet rot.

She whupped my arse with a yardstick fer near a hour wunst'n all I done wuz t'fuckin split a danged infinnytif.

Whut's a infinnytif?

Durned ifn I know, but round the marm I shore aint lettin on.

He can feel the rope suddenly giving way at last, just a few strands left uncut, but he has to pause when one of the revelers comes lumbering back into the dark to piss in the trough. It's the bald-headed preacher with the eye stitched through with a scar. His collar is turned the right way around now, but everything else is on backwards, causing him difficulties at the trough. He's staggering drunk, doesn't even seem to see him there. I'd like t'split *her* infinnytif, he bellows out, letting go above his belt and splattering just about everything except the trough.

Keerful, podnuh, someone calls out from the circle around the lamp. Yu're crossin inta perilous country.

Naw, I mean it, growls the parson, heading back, still dribbling down his leg, to join the others. Some of the rope strands seem to have grown back as tough as tendons and to be feeding on the blood leaking from his sliced behind. There's no time to lose. Yu wanta know the truth, I'd like t'rassle her down and fuck the bejesus outa her smartass ass.

Whoa, yu're talkin bout the schoolmarm, revrend! Yu're talkin about sumbody pure as the lily a the lake, sumbody as spotless and innercent as a angel in heaven!

But aint thet the more consarned reason? I mean, we're out here in the goddam Terrortory, boys, whut's lilies a the lake got t'do with it? Fuck it! I say we go fer her!

Them's mighty brave words, podnuh. I got dibs on seconds. Who's goin first?

There's a prevailing silence around the kerosene lamp, broken finally by a low stuttering fart. Yu volunteerin or whut? someone asks. Nope, nope! Thet one jest slipped out. As do his wrists, the tenacious snarl of bonds defeated at last. He unbuckles the belt, crawls out of the feeding trough, now swarming with writhing rope ends, and, hobbling on his bad leg, makes his way cautiously over to where the horses are. Well, someone says, it's the sheriff's fuckin party, lets use him t'break the marm in.

Aint we already done thet?

Not as I kin recollect, pard.

But didnt we—?

Yu callin me a liar?

No, no! Yu're right, I dont recollect neither. Let's git him.

This proposal meets with universal approval, expressed in meaty grunts, so he knows he has to keep moving, though moving's just what's most hard to do. He feels like he's wallowing agonizingly through thick mud just to cross the stable, and climbing up on the first horse he comes to is beyond his present abilities. Hey! Whar is he? he hears someone shout. He's gone! *Whut*—? A terrible weariness overtakes him and he fears all his heroics may have been for nothing, but the prospect of having to rape the schoolmarm and marry the chanteuse spurs him on, and, sucking air through his mouth, he silently eases the animal out of its stall. Thar he is! Over by the hosses! With the last of his strength he heaves himself headfirst over the horse's back and, whacking its rump with his hat and gunbelt and screaming like he's lost his reason, he sends it galloping madly out of the stable and into the desert night.

❧   ❧   ❧

At midday, he's still limply rag-dolled over the horse, his shredded butt baking in the sun and feasted on by flies. Hurts too much to move it. Hurts all over. His ribs are now as sore as the rest of him after the long frantic gallop out of town, and his back feels like it's broken. But at least he's gone from that place. For good, he hopes. About the long night, he remembers little after the shouts and gunfire. Instead, he recalls another night on the desert, long ago, when he was still adrift and in the saddle and had not yet reached the town, which was then nothing more than a teasing irregularity on the daytime horizon. He'd been moseying along for some time and had grown accustomed to the bleak austerity of that horizon and of the empty desert he was crossing, but on this particular night it seemed even more devoid of living feature than usual. Not a single cactus, no Joshua trees, sagebrush, or even scrub. No tumbleweeds. No water. Just rock and sand, as far as he could see, a vast dead thing spread out all about him beneath the alien immensity of the star-scattered sky, that lifeless beyond beyond this lifeless beyond, where, with what he has of a life, he'd come to. A desolate silence lay upon the stony plain as though compressed and baled and weightily stacked upon it, not so much as a whisper of a wind, nothing but the hollow clocklike clopping of his mustang's hoofs, he and the horse the only things in all this emptiness that moved.

Until, as he watched, the stars began to slide about, to realign themselves upon the black canvas of the sky as though to spell out some message for him. A warning maybe. But it was all just a sluggish scramble, like the shuffling of dominoes, nothing he could make any sense of, and he grasped thereby some small portion of his fate: that anything the universe might have to say would remain forever incomprehensible to him. So, well, maybe he could read what they had to say after all.

While gazing up at this display, he stumbled upon an old toothless Indian sitting alone on a flat stone before a small heap of glowing red embers. Nearly trod on him before he saw him there, a medicine man by the looks of him, though it could just as well have been an old squaw with shriveled dugs. This person, also staring up at the swarm of stars overhead while sucking on a long-stemmed pipe, made no sign of greeting but did not seem surprised that he'd come upon him or her in this manner. Whut do they say, oletimer? he asked. Whut do the stars say? The Indian slowly turned his or her head and peered at him, seated up there on his mustang like something growing out of its back. After a long silent time, the Indian said: They say the universe is mute. Only men speak. Though there is nothing to say. Then the ancient turned away and fell silent again, tending the embers, whose whole purpose seemed to be to provide for the relighting of the pipe from time to time. Probably would have been better if he'd let it go at that and continued on his way. Instead, he traded a strip of buffalo jerky for a few puffs on the pipe, and the next thing he knew everything was spinning around (now he could read the sky; it was like a kaleidoscopic shuffle of dirty pictures going on up there) and the old Indian was making off with his horse and all his goods. Though he was seeing double, he managed to bring the thieving savage down with a single shot to the back of his head as he was galloping away by firing both pistols at the same time. He wasn't sure if both bullets made the same hole or if he'd shot two Indians, but he didn't stay around to figure it out, being fairly spooked by now by the astral spectacles he was witnessing. He whistled his mustang back and heaved himself up into the saddle (it was as though he had shrunk some, it was like climbing a mountain, and he had the impression that the horse helped him somehow) and, arms wrapped round its thick neck, he made his way away, head down, from that wild stony place. It was probably about then that the ache to get back to civilization set in.

Of which by now he's had his fill. Something to be said for the desert after all. His view of it, draped butt-high over the back of the horse, an old trailworn snuff-colored cayuse, is mostly of the ground passing under the creature's plodding hoofs, and it strikes him that survival in the desert probably depends on attending fiercely to such details and avoiding the long view of the horizon, which can suck the gaze right out of a person's eyes. The horizon's a sight he suffers but rarely now, and then only upside down from under the horse's belly whenever his head bobs in that direction. It's a disconcerting perspective, making him feel suddenly untethered, having to hold on to the horse's rough hairy body not to fall backwards into the sky, so he often closes his eyes when it bobs into view. And it is with his eyes closed like that in dread of being roofed by the barren desert that he hears nearby the muffled cry of a woman.

He rears up in surprise and falls off the horse. This hurts considerably, especially through the middle parts, though it's fuzzed in with all his other hurts, pain being mostly what his body's made of at this time. He lies there on the stony ground for a moment, curled up, doubting he'll ever be able to straighten out again, listening to the woman's rodentlike whimpering, but not for long; he hasn't come across many women out in these parts and so is sufficiently provoked by the very novelty of it to raise himself up and have a look. It's the village schoolmarm, bound and gagged on the ground a few paces away from him, measuring in the old manner from a time when he could still walk. Now he crawls toward her on his belly, sidling his way over like a broken snake might. Yu awright, mam? he gasps.

She glares at him, struggling against her bonds. Her wrists and ankles are hogtied behind her back and her gaping mouth is stretched wide around a reddish sweat stained neckerchief, much like one he used to have, knotted tightly behind her ears. Clumsied by his own injuries and his shyness, he fumbles with the kerchief, but she shakes her head and jerks her body at him, grunting urgently now and glancing fearfully off toward the horizon, as though there might be no time to lose. He tries to turn her over on her stomach, but she seems pinned fast to the ground: he raises one hip out of the way and sees that she is lashed to what look like traces of old rusted railroad tracks, buried in the sand. He brushes the sand away to get at the knots and feels her supple flesh beneath the black dress bounce back against his hands and then stiffly recoil. Beggin yer pardon, mam, he says, and brushes away a bit more, his pains subsiding. She takes one sniff of him, glances at the filthy pink bloomers, and turns away in disgust, looking as if she might throw up. He has to reach under her to get at the knots that have parceled up her hands and feet, the ropes tough as plant roots and buried deep, and it is only after he has been working on them for a time that he registers fully just where his hands are, for he has not thought soberly upon the schoolmarm's bottom before, nor the place down there of the parting of her thighs, now pocketing his busy raw-knuckled fists, even though he does have some notion of the black webbed tangle it might be wrapped in, got from some former time. When, to get at a rope end, he burrows a bit deeper, she arches her back away from his hands in alarm, bumping his knees with her belly, but he means her no harm, nor has he any desire to take advantage of her, for he thinks of her as the most innocent and virtuous creature on earth, and even her bottom is not so much a bottom in his mind as the pedestal from which, straight-backed and true, her virtue rises. Just where that notion of a rising pedestal has come from, of course, is all too manifest, given the split and tattered condition of Belle's bloomers, and he turns his backside to the marm so as not to abuse her with the plain and miserable sight of it. Sorry, mam, he says, unsheathing his bowie knife and straddling her, but them knots is too tight to untangle, I'm gonna hafta cut em. So hole still, I dont want yu gittin poked.

Her eyes widen at the sight of the knife (in truth, though the question has been on his mind all night, he can't tell what color they are, for what he sees mostly is the piercing blackness of the pupils), and she goes limp. Even her bottom feels more like a bottom now to the back of his hand as he grips her four fettered limbs down there to hold them steady, and her half-raised hip, which his member is stiffly grazing as though to plow a furrow in it, is a womanly hip in spite of its thick black wrap, pliant and gently rounded, a comfort to his gaze and to his touch. He works the blade carefully in under the ropes between her wrists and ankles, grateful for the time it takes, then with a single upward stroke severs them. The rope ends shrivel back into the sand and the train tracks disappear, but his fullest attention is on the schoolmarm, who seems—so pale and tearful, a limp bundle of the most immaculate and vulnerable softness—too faint to rise. He staggers to his feet, his manhood wagging cheerfully in the blazing sun, not much he can do about that, and tenderly lifts her up, just as a train comes roaring up out of the far horizon and goes thundering past, knocking him back with the mighty violence of its passage. And then as soon as it has come it is gone again. He can hear it bearing away into the distance and as though wheeling around some bend he cannot see, and then he cannot hear it any longer. He sets the marm down and, still gazing off toward the empty horizon, cuts away the rag that gags her. If thet warnt the dangedest thing I ever seen, he says.

Saw, she replies sharply, spitting the gag away, and she slaps him. A real cracker that makes his teeth rattle. Then she mounts his horse sidesaddle and leaves him there, alone on the empty desert, without another word. He rubs his cheek, watching her as she quickly diminishes and then vanishes over the horizon. Never could understand women.

⚜   ⚜   ⚜

His face is still stinging from the schoolmarm's slap when the town rolls up under his feet again and the saloon chanteuse leans out of an upstairs window to holler down: Whuddayu doin back here, stranger? I thought yu'd skedaddled. Yer mug's up all over town!

Reckon I jest caint stay away, he says drily. It's true, he sees his face on WANTED posters nailed up everywhere, though the one hung on the jailhouse hitching rail over by the old buckboard is more like a rear view of his desperate escape from the stables: HOSS THIEF! it says. REEWARD! DAID OR KICKIN! Except for the orange-haired chanteuse framed by her lace-curtained window, there is no sign of life in the dusty town, nor even a hot wind to stir the gallows ropes or rock the saloon signs. It is empty and silent, yet everything seems tautly edged in the shadowless light of high noon as if the whole town were mined with dynamite. He's in no shape to draw on anybody, but his hands are tensed over his gunbelt out of an old gunfighter's habit, which is the only habit he respects. Whar is everbody? he asks.

Dunno. Probly out lookin fer yu, badman. Guess thet wuz some damn stag party. I must say yu do look mighty appealin, standin out thar in the street with yer weepon stickin out like yu wuz aimin t'ambush us all. Mebbe I should oughter come down thar'n hang my wet pussy on it a spell, jest so's it dont git dried out in the sun.

Well I wuz wonderin ifn mebbe yu still had my britches sumwhars.

I think I seen em about. Stay whar yu are, honey. I'll hunt fer em'n brang em down.

Staying where he is, there in the middle of his own portrait gallery, makes no practical sense, and he anticipates Belle might have notions about that reward money or else further marital designs, but in a wide-open ramshackle town like this, made out of a few boards and a bit of tin, it's not easy to find a place to hole out in unnoticed. What he settles on finally is his own jailhouse, where he might best defend himself until everything gets explained. So he limps heavily over there, dragging his bad leg behind him like a laden travois, and finds them all inside waiting for him. They kick his feet out from under him, strip him of his weapons, and give him a thorough hiding with their fists and boots, gun butts and wooden legs.

We'da hung yu straight off, yu dodrabbid no-good thievin varmint, but on accounta yu wuz wunst a lawman, yu'll git a trial, fair'n square, and then we'll hang yu.

Dont do me no favors, he groans, and rolls over to hug his pain, and they kick him some more. He feels like he's breathing directly through a cold painful hole in his chest, and he notices then that he's no longer wearing his badge. Must have fallen off back in the stables. Or maybe before. Can't remember when last he saw it.

They drag him by his feet to a cell and heave him in, but there's another person in there. Looks to have been dead for three or four weeks. When he points this out to them, a bespectacled old humpback, who might once have been his deputy, one of them anyway, kicks at the body and says: Musta been a malfeasant some other sheriff roped. Fergot t'feed him, I reckon. They pick up the corpse and throw it out into the street and then they lock him up in there and hang the key on the far wall, which is otherwise covered with the photographs of dead people, everything from hollow-eyed babies to bullet-ridden bandits and heaped-up massacre victims.

The present deputy, a tall ugly man with long greasy hair like knotted iron rope and a random scattering of gold teeth, settles into a creaky swivel chair with a pipe and bottle and deck of cards while the other men clamber out into the darkness, headed for the saloon and arguing about how the reward money is to be divvied up. What he regrets now, curled up there on the cell floor, is that he didn't hop that train when it roared through. Wasn't thinking. Not about that. What a woman will do to you. Not that it would have made much difference. One night after a saloon bust-up, he recalls, he got thrown into jail with a famous trainrobber due to hang at dawn. In the town whar I growed up, the trainrobber told him, they wuz all this fuckin storifyin. Yu couldnt hardly git clear of it. I wuz afeerd I'd hafta spend my whole goddam life insida cock'n bull cooked up by other people. Mostly dead people. So thet's why I come out here. Yarn my own dyin, as yu might say. Well pears like yu done it, he said, for he was young and wild then and he admired the man. The trainrobber, however, stared at him like he was the village idiot. Like fuckin hell, he said.

He's still there on the floor and growing used to it when the saloon chanteuse turns up with a clay crock full of baked beans. Aint he a purty mess, she says, looking in on him. Them duds is plain revoltin. Take em off him, deppity, I'll warsh em up fer his hangin exhibit.

I aint touchin them filthy bloomers, Belle.

Yu dont hafta. Jest git me his hat and boots and thet buckskin shirt.

The deputy scratches his armpits thoughtfully, then hollers at him: Shuck them duds, yu jasper, and throw em out here fore I shoot yer fuckin ass off!

Go t'hell, he mutters, and the deputy lets off a shot that burns his ear. Probably put a hole in it.

Keerful, deppity. Yu'll spoil him fer the hangin. Open up, I'll git them things off him.

Yu wouldnt be pullin nuthin funny, would yu, Belle?

I'd like t'pull his funny little nuthin out by the ruts, deppity, ifn thet's whut yu mean. This here's the two-timin dog whut left me standin at the altar—yu wuz thar, yu seen it. Hell, I caint wait t'see the shifty sumbitch swing. Now open up'n lemme at him.

Humph. Awright, he says. He can hear the key clanking in the lock. But I'm keepin my gun on yu alla same.

Well jest dont open up no new holes, I caint find enuf hard men in this town t'service the ones I got. She sets the dish of beans on the floor and kneels down beside him, flashing her naked under- parts at him. I brung yu sumthin t'eat, honey, she says suggestively, and the thing between her legs seems to blow him a wet kiss. He turns his head away. Yes, there has definitely been some damage done to that ear. The chanteuse straddles his legs to work his boots off and massages herself on the hairy parts there, then unbuckles his gunbelt and pulls his shirt off over his head. Yu're really up agin it, hero, she whispers, breathing heavily. Yu got more troubles than a rat-tailed hoss tied short in flytime.

I'm glad t'hear it. I wuz afeerd everthin wuz gonna be awright. Whuddayu sayin t'him, Belle?

I tole him he wuz a rat fer stealin thet hoss and he'd be flyin high in short time. Now yu jest dig inta them beans, short-timer, and wait here till I brang these things back t'yu.

I aint goin nowhars.

Yu bet yer ass yu aint, says the deputy, locking up again. The chanteuse, he sees, has her free hand in the deputy's pants.

Yu're near as ugly down thar, deppity, as yu are up top, she says.

I know it. Yu hankerin fer a poke, Belle?

Aint I always, she moans, nuzzling in under his spidery hair to chew on a thick lump of scar tissue that was probably once part of an ear. Yu go on playin with thet piece a gristle, deppity, and keep it lively till I git back with the kid's duds.

She seems to go out the door and come right back in again, though it's not like that, he knows, because meanwhile he's found the hacksaw in the pot of beans and has been removing the window bars while his keeper's had his back turned, sucking from his whiskey bottle and playing solitaire by lamplight. The bars, he's discovered, are just old wooden fenceposts tarred black; he could have punched them out.

He drops the hacksaw back into the crock of beans as the deputy rises boozily from his chair and staggers over to unlock the cell. Yu got a awful purty stink about yu tonight, Belle.

Well yu kin have a lick in a minnit, deppity. Jest lemme git these here togs back on thet scoundrel, I'm sicka seein him walk around near stark nekkid like thet. It aint civvylized.

His buckskins, he sees, have been dyed black. They wuz too dirty to warsh, she explains, I hadta color em. She has also brought him a broad slouch hat, gloves, neckerchief, and boots, all black as well. Even the longjohns are black. She peels the tattered pink bloomers off him and tosses them out the cell door: Here, go sniff these whilst yu're waitin, deppity! The man, cross-eyed with drink, catches them, peers at them woozily, turns green, and stumbles out the door to vomit in the street. While he's gone, the chanteuse, tugging the longjohns up and snuggling his bruised eggs in with particular tenderness, whispers: They's a hoss and weapons waitin fer yu outside thet winder, darlin. Now haul the resta yer livery on and git outa here whilst me'n the deppity says our prayers. I'll meet up with yu later.

But whar—?

Dont worry, handsome, she grins. I'll find yu. Yu caint git lost.

✧   ✧   ✧

A lot of things happen and then he's alone and forsaken on the desert again, sprawled out under the black canopy of night, starving, parched, hurting too much to get up and move on but a dead man if he doesn't. Not a calamity out in these parts of course, the more serious concern being the loss of his hat and boots on the wild gallop out of town on the back of the black mare. That creature, after effecting one rescue, has tossed him here and abandoned him, flat out, useless, and in need of another, on what an old furtrapper come down out of the mountains once called the dry skin of the ineffable, which back then he thought was a Sunday way of saying the unfuckable.

One of the things that happened was that, while Belle serviced the drunken deputy behind his desk (We dont want thet wild desperado gittin over-roused, do we, she said with a wink his way, pushing the ugly man down out of sight), he picked up his boots and crawled out of the cell window, which turned out to be a story higher in the back than out front; he could see the horse waiting for him down below with his gunbelt over its rump, so he just let go and dropped, slapping into the saddle like a ball into a leather glove. It hurt but not as much as he'd feared, though probably the most recent punishments he'd endured had set new standards. But if the horse, a shapely coal-black thoroughbred, was willing to play catch with him, she was less inclined to take him anywhere, impassively ignoring his most desperate urgings. He wheedled, kneed her, clucked his tongue in her ear, snapped the reins, commanded her in a barking whisper to giddyup, smacked her haunches, and cursed her like the black devil she was, but she only turned her head and looked at him wistfully, or else in reproach or disappointment.

Over at the saloon meanwhile a brawl had broken out, a fight over the reward money as best he could make out, or maybe they'd been gambling for it and someone had cheated, and it was now spilling out into the street. There were fistfights and gunfire and thrown bottles and chairs and the shattering of windows and mirrors and, mixed in with it all, a drunken agitation for a lynching boiling up: It's thet goddamn hoss-thievin ex-sheriff whut's fucked us up! Lets go drag the mizzerbul whelp outa thar'n string him up! Yo! He's ruint this town! C'mon! Lets git the sumbitch! But still, even as the turmoil spread ominously in his direction, the mare just stood there, stock-still, eyeing him melancholically over her shoulder, and he began to wonder if maybe the saloon chanteuse, more embittered by her thwarted wedding party than she was letting on, had set him up for something even more harrowing than a legal hanging. Git goin, damn yu! he cried, but the contrary thing wouldn't. He felt like braining her with something, but she was all he had so he gritted his teeth and leaned forward and stroked her sleek black neck and begged her earnestly to fetch him out of this hellatious dusthole before it was too late, whispering in her erected ear that it was just the two of them now, his fate was in her hands—or hoofs, better said—and if she wanted to stay and get killed like a damfool, well, he could abide by that, for him it was better to get shot up out here in the street than to swing like sausage from a rope, but there was no need for her to suffer such grievous shit, no need for either of them to, because there was still time and plenty, but they had to step lively—and pronto!—and as he talked she began to paw the ground and snort and toss her head and he told her she was the most beautiful horse he'd ever seen but he wouldn't care if she were the ugliest whangdoodle in all creation, he'd still love her, if only she would kick up her heels and hightail her sweet arse out of here, and the next thing he knew they were miles away, streaking through the desert night so fast it was all he could do to hold his seat, his eyelids pinned back, teeth bared behind blown-open lips, the new hole in his ear whistling, his clothes ripping in the wind. Then, as suddenly, they stopped and he somersaulted right on over the mare's head with his forward momentum, landing where he lies now, flat on his back, staring up at the indifferent stars, hatless, bootless, unarmed, and unable to imagine ever rising again, the mercurial black mare long since vanished into the night, as though, having brought him this far and dropped him, her job was done.

Well, he's been thrown off horses before. Breaking broncs is part of who he is, what he does. Or used to be, do, best he can recollect, his memory about this residing mostly at the base of his spine and now freshly jogged. But it's been awhile. That mustang he rode in here was probably the last one he broke. If he ever really did. Wasn't easy. It had been living wild and had acquired fixed notions about anybody sitting upon it. Which, not caring to be sat upon himself, he could respect, but only up to the point where it started to hurt. That horse would stand still as stone and then would suddenly unwind like a clock spring, throwing a body every which direction, no two of its feet hitting the grit at the same time. It whirled, sunfished, high-dived, and back-flipped; it was like riding the end of a whip or trying to cling to a cliff face in an earthquake. With the cheeks of your backside. He got bucked into mud holes, cactus patches, manure wagons, and bonfires, once even up a tree. And he got mad. Goddammit, it was either him or the horse. He had himself lashed to the stirrups and saddle with the intention of riding it all day and all night for as long as it took. How long that was he can't say, but it seemed like a lifetime, a bone-breaking nightmare that would never end. He came to one day at the bottom of a ravine in a pile of brambles, still tied to the busted tack and the horse quietly grazing on the hillside overhead.

The horse had bested him but they got on after that. Partners of a sort. Neither of them went back to where they'd been; he wouldn't have known how to find his way back had he wanted to. Instead, they just kept moving, a pair of fiddle-footed ramblers, following the wind, until that drifting brought them out here. To the desert. Where now, somewhere, a coyote yaps and a lone wolf howls. A not too subtle reminder. That he's meat. And the desert's dry belly on which he lies is hollow and full of a restless insatiable hunger. Even now he feels that belly rumbling faintly beneath him, hears it: *some animal stealthily approaching.* He has no weapons, not even his bowie knife, but whatever it is will not get a free meal. He lies deadly still, trying to estimate how far away it is and just where it's coming from, sniffing the air for a clue, gazing fixedly up at the night sky, wishing it were a mirror. No movement up there tonight, the stars are all nailed in their places, but they are flickering as if they might be loose and could easily fall out. He concentrates on them, as though he might unplug one with his gaze alone. And then, to his startlement (he cries out) he does, or seems to, but it misses his predator and lands on him instead. But: not a star. No. He's been hit in the face with a boot, his own boot. Standing over him is the black mare. She's come back. Her coat is wet with sweat and there is foam at the corners of her mouth. She drops the other boot, his hat, his gunbelt, the sheathed knife.

He lies back, staring up at this giant of a horse above him, her black body blotting out the stars, but her own eyes luminous as moons, and he feels suddenly more attached to the earth than he's ever felt before. It's as though the horse, whom he has sorely misjudged, without explaining anything (he's as ignorant as he ever was), has given him a reason for being, and a desire for it too, and he knows now they will survive this night. She bends down, rubs her broad nose against his, nuzzles his chest as if to encourage him to get on with it. Yes, he knows they have to keep moving, they've probably followed her here, but the harmonious view he has of the universe at this moment is so compelling he wants to hold on to it for a moment longer. He feels that he is gazing, gazing up at the horse and the sky, upon truth itself, the core and essence of it. Ineffable of course, like the smelly old fellow said, aghast at what he saw, but his heart, his most unexercised organ, is touched. He reaches up in gratitude to stroke the mare's neck, but she flinches and jerks back. What—? Blood! She's been wounded! They've shot at her, those vicious yellow-livered cabbageheads! The rage that wells up in him serves a purpose: it stirs him to sit up and don the gunbelt and the other things she's brought him. He's ready to take them all on! She watches patiently, nosing the ground as if to graze there, though there's nothing to eat. The boots are the hardest. He doesn't bend well and his strength is gone. She sets a foot by his to give him something to push against. That much done, he tries to rise, holding on to her shoulder, gets as far as his knees, but cannot seem to manage the rest. If he plants one foot on the ground, the other gives way. She solves this problem too. She picks him up with her teeth by the seat of his pants and lifts him up onto her back, which he clumsily falls upon, spread out on his belly and legs adangle. So much for taking on the world. She whinnies softly. He hugs her neck, and together they gallop away from there.

✦　✦　✦

He is not much of a dreamer. When he's awake he's awake, and when he sleeps he sleeps. But this night on the desert, collapsed over the back of the galloping black mare, he dreams he is traveling in a stagecoach with a beautiful woman in black who is twice his size. They are passing through dangerous country full of Indians and bandits, and she is telling him a story about a brave, resourceful, and adventurous youth on a perilous journey into a demonic wasteland. He was honest and strong, possessed of a preponderance of muscular development and animal spirits, she tells him, with square iron-cast shoulders and limbs like bars of steel. He tries to picture this, while she turns, showing him the black beauty spot in her cheek, to peer wistfully out the stagecoach window as though the beautiful youth might be out there somewhere. The stagecoach is being attacked, but somehow they are only spectators. He had golden curly hair and a manly brow, she goes on softly, turning back to him, and he had sparkling blue eyes, which were tender and soulful in repose, but firm and determined under excitement. His aquiline nose was as straight as an arrow and as if chiseled from the finest Parian marble, and he had a square jaw and cleft chin and a perfect set of even white teeth, which gleamed when he smiled like rows of lustrous pearls. She smiles faintly as though to demonstrate this pearly luster, though in fact her mouth is full of shadows. He did not take advantage of his superior strength, nor use it without considerable provocation, and then only in a fair competition. And he was always chivalrous toward women. They are completely surrounded now by Indians or bandits or both and the ride in the rocking stagecoach is getting rougher, the wooden wheels slamming against the ruts and stones and bouncing high and coming down again with a rattling jar, the leather springs squealing, bullets and arrows pimpling the paneling. He believed that he was independent and free and in control of his own destiny, she adds, sorrow clouding her face, but of course he was merely an agent of fate. And on top of that, she sighs, he is dead. Dead? he asks. He wants to crawl up on her lap and be hugged, but her hands are folded there. The coach driver up top, she says. Haven't you been paying attention? He's dead. The horses are out of control.

That's why they are going so fast and heaving about so wildly. He knows he must prove his own courage and resourcefulness; it may even be why they have undertaken this harrowing journey. He crawls down off the seat and opens the coach door. It tears away with their violent speed, sweeping several attackers off their horses as a thrown wooden block might knock down toy cavalrymen. It is not easy to reach the driver's seat; he must work his way up the side of the speeding stagecoach, hand over hand, grasping the window frames and moldings and railings and brass fittings, and many times he is nearly flung off. Clinging to the lurching coach is like riding a wild horse, and he realizes that he may be the only person in the world who can do this. All the while, gunshots and arrows slam into the side of the coach, narrowly missing him or perhaps even hitting him, he can't be sure, nor does he much care; he doesn't expect to get out of this alive, he just wants to get the next thing done.

The driver's seat atop the express box is vacant and then it is not: a man looms high above him with burning eyes and rough grizzled chops. He is shouting at the thundering team of horses—*hi! hi!*— and lashing them with a long black whip, driving them ever faster. The driver seems to know that he is there, crawling up the side of the coach, but he pretends not to see him. This cannot be the real driver. The bandits or Indians must have killed the real one. Whom he loved, or may have loved (if he knew him). *Hi!* cries the wild-eyed driver and cracks his whip. Though he has reached only the height of the driver's knees, he somehow wrests the whip away from him. The driver shrinks away from him in terror as he raises the whip over his head—he seems to be standing a yard or two in front of him, as if on a platform over the first pair of horses—and then he snaps the whip and with a single stroke whisks the driver's head clean off: it flies away, bouncing off the top of the stagecoach, with a look of blind amazement. He turns to grab up the reins but there are no reins, and the runaway horses are at full gallop, hauling the careening stagecoach toward a yawning precipice. Beside him on the seat, the driver's headless body rocks stiffly from side to side, hammering his shoulder as if trying to knock him off the box and get back at him for taking his head off. He would jump from the doomed coach, but the lady in black is still down inside, so he has to stop it somehow before they reach the precipice. The only way he knows to do that is to crawl forward to the lead horses and rein them in. Without hesitation, he throws himself down on the first pair of horses below him, but he misses and falls between them into the tackle that conjoins them, which for some reason he associates with garter belts. He wants to rise and make his way to the front, but he is somewhat entangled, and the rhythm of the team's galloping hoofs is lulling him to sleep. As he's drifting off, the woman in black joins him down there in the tackle. It's all right, she says, stroking his forehead (with her nose?). It's not your fault. And she stretches out beside him, cradled there amid the thundering hoofs, and, at peace with himself at last (the precipice? it's nothing, forget it), he drops off, snuggled safely up against her.

When he awakens, he is not sure at first from what he is waking or whose might be the warm body against which he's pressed. He keeps his eyes closed for a moment to retain something of the comforting aura of the dream before the hard world overtakes him again, the sense it gave him of knowing who he is and why he's here, but in fact that aura has faded away and all that's left is the memory of being at the edge of something (some woman?) and the look on the grizzled old furtrapper's face when he told him he was the only person in the world who could do this. He's not even sure he was himself in the dream, it was like he was somebody else, someone who was taking him somewhere he didn't want to go. Which makes no sense. Hanging on to dreams is like trying to eat a smell. Everything is so vivid and real and full of significance at the time, but afterwards only these dim ghostly images remain to haunt the woken head.

Well well. Mornin, sunshine. He opens his eyes a slit. It's the saloon chanteuse standing in the doorway. Some doorway or other. Yu two sleep well?

He's lying on a rancid old mattress with straw ticking and rags for blankets, but it's more easeful than the desert floor or a jolting saddle, to which he is more accustomed, and he has slept hard. And long: must be the middle of the day. His companion in the bed is the black mare, lying on her side with her back to him. He rolls away from her and sits up, still trying to recall the dream, but it's mostly gone. Can't remember how he got here, either. *Here* being a dilapidated wooden shack, badly shot up and with half the roof gone. His boots and buckskins have been removed; he's wearing only a black union suit and a neckerchief.

I wuz havin a dream about my father, he says with a precipitous yawn, as the mare rolls heavily out of the bed behind him and clops outside to do her morning business.

Do tell. Nice feller?

Dunno. Never knowed him.

The chanteuse, standing in the noonday sunlight coming through the roof, is rigged out today in a fancy black outfit of her own: shirt and short knee-length skirt with beads and fringes, high boots, six-shooters on her hips, and a flat black hat with little crimson tassels hanging from the stiff brim, matching the ruby in her cheek. I mean in the dream, she says.

Caint recollect. I think he tried t'kill me.

Musta been him, awright. But git yer boots on, cowboy. Dont want the lawr t'ketch yu here.

Caint think how I got em off. Whar we goin?

She puts a black mask on over her eyes and hands him one like it. Yu're a famous badman now, darlin. So we gotta round us up a gang a sneakthiefs, gunslingers, and short-iron specialists and go do some killin and robbin.

While waiting to waylay a train that night, he and his band of outlaws, all hard men wearing black hats, sit around a campfire on top of the railway tracks they've scouted out, while the orange-haired chanteuse, now a bandit queen and perched high on the day's pile of loot, sings them sentimental old ballads about lost solitude and soiled doves and tipi-burning in the untrodden vales of purple sage, and about dirty dealing and dysentery and wick-dipping in the old corral with its rivers of blood flowing beneath the whispering cottonwood trees. They've been out robbing stores and banks and killing people all day and they're all a bit trail-weary, grateful for this restful interlude, and when Belle sings about the hanging judge who hanged a whole town, they all sing along (even he joins in, though he can't sing a lick) as she lists the victims, each verse adding two or three more—He hung the teacher and the preacher and the Chinese prostitute! He hung the rambler and the gambler and the pegleg in his boot!—then in unison shout out the chorus: *But he never hung me!* And they laugh and spit at the fire and pass the whiskey bottles, reckless violent men of good spirit.

His black mare is curled up beside him by the fire, allowing herself to be used as a backrest and a shield against the elements. The place they have come to is bald and open to the four winds, which are all active on the night, blowing dust up their noses and whipping their hats off. They have to keep an eye on the campfire that blown embers don't set the dry scrub ablaze and spoil their robbery plans, but they need the light from it so as not to lose sight of the train rails, which have been eluding them all day, slippery as watersnakes. It has taken hours hunting them down to this lonely spot, and then thanks mainly to his black mare who led them here, following a spoor of fine cinder, after the rails they'd been tracking had seemingly dead-ended in a waterhole. Even here, the rails have tried to slither away, which is why they've built their campfire on top of them: if they shift again, they'll all shift together.

Most commonly after so long in the saddle, getting his thighs buffed and his prostate spanked all day, he's pretty sore, finding sitting down and standing up equally insufferable, but the mare is an easy ride and if anything he feels better tonight than when the day began, no new torments and his old wounds and bruises mainly healed as though gently massaged and oiled away. She's fast, too, and fearless, coolly outrunning the bullets shot at them today as they galloped away from trouble, and she can fly over fences and chasms, take any incline or crisis in her stride, turn on a nickel and leave four cents' change. They had to kill a few breachy clerks, shopkeepers, and deputy sheriffs during the day's adventures, but the only serious trouble they had was when they were robbing black hats from a dry goods emporium and ran into another gang robbing the same store. During the explosive shootout that erupted, the mare slipped in and stole all the hats, rescued him from where he was pinned down behind the calico bolts, and, stomping a few heads along the way, led the whole gang in a clean getaway. Almost clean. They lost a couple of men to the hail of fire, but members of the rival bunch later offered to join up with them if they could have a hat, so they are back to a full complement again.

Now one of the new members of the gang, a rangy white-shirted and black-vested dude with muttonchops, sleeve garters, and spectacles like two dimes on a wire, interrupts the bandit queen's legs-up number about skylarking range tramps on a bunk-house toot to complain that his hat doesn't fit him properly. It sets down on my ears sorta funnylike, he grumbles.

Dodblast yer peculiar pitcher, growls a black-bearded hunch-back, and he pulls out his walnut-handled pistol and shoots the man square between the dimes. Belle wuz singin.

Hole on thar, Bible back, says a swarthy squint-eyed fat man with a cigarillo dangling in his scarred puffy lips. Thet feller was a pal a mine. Yu didnt hafta kill him jest on accounta he busted in on a fuckin song.

No? The hunchback turns his pistol on the fat man. Yu want yer turn, buzzardbait?

The fat man squints expressionlessly down the barrel of the pistol, dragging slowly on the cigarillo, his hands tensed on his knees. Yu rather hold over me, podnuh. I reckon I caint call thet hand. Ash blows from the reddening cigarillo in the coiling wind. Ante'n pass the buck.

The buck aint fer passin, puffguts, and the ante's yer ass, says the bearded hunchback, cocking the hammer of his pistol.

He gets up from where he's been lying against the black mare, walks over there, ready to shoot them both if he has to, at the same time that the bandit queen climbs down off the pile of loot and interposes herself between them, her tasseled sombrero tipped sternly down over one brow as if to say she means business. We aint got time fer no hossshit bickerin, boys, she says, cuffing their ears so sharply she knocks their hats off. He reaches down and takes the hunchback's gun away from him, uncocks it, empties the chamber, drops it back in his lap. Now I want yu two bigmouth jackasses t'shake'n make up.

Aw Belle. . . .

C'mon now, aint no point argufyin the question, she says, giving them another slap. Thet train's due by here any minnit. Yu in this gang or aint yu?

Ow! Shore, Belle, but—

Then git to it.

Well. Well awright, dammit, I'm sorry I shot yer bud. It wuz jest I wuz so wound up awaitin fer thet cussed train.

It dont matter none. T'tell the truth I couldnt hardly suffer thet dandified turkeyass anyhow.

Thet's a whole sight better, boys, says the bandit queen, ruffling their hair, and she climbs back up on the loot and tunes up her guitar, while he rests down against the mare again, fingering the gold ring that Belle stole earlier for the bullet hole in his ear and reflecting, as he watches the stars get whipped about by the winds, on the way his own days seem to blow past him out here as though on those winds, and his memory of them, too, swept away as if they never were, leaving only a lingering constellation of habits and impressions that constitutes his dim untidy notion of himself; and constellations, as a crusty old scout once pointed out to him, do not really exist but are merely the local illusion of earthbound ramblers. That's what he said, and it seems likely so. Which means he knows nothing, and sometimes less than that when confusions beset him. One impression that the day has given him, for example, is that he probably takes more favorably to breaking the law than to preserving it, but that preference is muddied by a troubling disquiet of the heart, the nature of which he suspects but cannot quite take in, for he has always known himself to be—by trade, druthers, and constitution—a free man and a drifter and a loner, not susceptible to such perturbations. But all that was before he laid eyes on the town schoolmarm. He can still see her, tied to the railroad tracks, so sad and sweet and needful a creature wriggling around down there. In short, his constellated notion of himself be damned, he may well be (though that's just it, he can't be) in love, and here, astray outside the law, it's a love utterly denied him. Them rails hummin yet? Belle asks.

An eye-patched mestizo with long black greasy hair puts his one ear to the rail that he's been squatting on. Nope. Nuthin.

Mebbe these aint the right ones, says a bandy-legged old graybeard in a red undershirt and black derby. Mebbe these're jest more false tracks thet goldang train has laid down t'throw us offn its trail.

The black mare behind him lifts her head and shakes it with a dissentious snort. Them's the tracks, ole man, he says quietly, patting the mare's shoulder. Dont git antsy. It'll be here soon enuf.

To bide the waiting time and calm this restless bunch of high-tempered roadriders, Belle sings old campmeeting favorites about destiny and fast guns, potency and freedom (Sumthin howlin sumthin prowlin black'n hairy on the prairie, she warbles into the dark windy night, the ruby in her cheek so lit up from the campfire it seems more like a window to a furnace in her mouth), and at the end (Space without end! Aymen! Aymen!) he and the men all join in by throwing their heads back and emitting long mournful howls, which seem to enter into the winds and become part of them and spread over the dimly glowing landscape as though to blanket it with the foggy ache of their unrealized desires.

Slowly the howls fade into the distance, carried away by the departing winds, and in the dense silence that follows, the stringy-haired mestizo puts his ear to the tracks and raises his hand and whispers: It's comin!

Hastily, they stamp out the fire and don their masks and mount their horses: they can hear it now, wailing dolefully in the distance, as though returning their own howls, and heading this way. He steps the black mare into the middle of the track bed to block the train's passage and also to nail the skittery rails in place, and the others gather around him, pistols and rifles out, waiting for whatever happens next. The roar augments, the steam whistle bawls, they can hear the rhythmic clatter of the steel wheels drawing ever nearer, but as yet no sign of the train itself.

We should oughter be seein its light, someone says, and suddenly everything goes silent.

Whut—? Whar'd it go?

Sshh!

They stand there in the dead of night, huddled together on their horses atop the short stretch of rails they've secured, scanning the pale empty horizon, nothing to be heard but their own breathing and the occasional stamp of a hoof, someone sucking nervously on a loose tooth. And then, as suddenly as the silence fell, the train is thundering up on them, its whistle shrieking, its headlight swinging above them like a diabolical pendulum, fire belching from its stack, sparks flying from the pounding wheels. Horses rear, riders tumble, some scream and run, but he and the mare stand fast and the train vanishes again. Silence and darkness fall, even deeper than before.

While the other men, mumbling curses, brush themselves off and crawl back onto their horses, the bandit queen sidles up to him on her golden palomino and says: Whuddayu reckon?

Dunno. Must be hidin from us. Tryin to.

It aint got past?

No. It's out thar. Sumwhars. Slowly his eyes, temporarily blinded by the locomotive's headlamp, adjust to the darkness, and he searches the bleak scene for any irregularity which might conceal so great a thing. Mostly just dark clumps of sage, scrub, out-croppings of pale rocks.

Whut about thet ole abandoned silver mine?

Silver mine?

Over thar. In thet little cleft this side a thet far butte. See the black hole? It's deep and it's got rails down it coulda used.

He nods. Aint nuthin else t'choose from. He turns to the old graybeard. Yu stay here, oletimer, and mind them tracks dont sneak off sumwhars. The resta yu men come with me.

It's a fair gallop across the vast flat desert to the silver mine, but they cover it in due time, or rather in no time at all, for it seems he's still contemplating the distance they have to travel when they are pulling up at the mouth of the mine on sweaty frothing horses to ponder their next move.

It's down thar awright, whispers one of the men. I kin hear it wheezin.

So, uh, whuddawe gonna do, kid? It's the trigger-happy hump-back, now wearing the wire-rimmed specs on his bulbous nose, the two black disks pupilled each by a reflected star.

Pears we got no choice. The train's gone down thet hole. Ifn we wanta rob it, we gotta go down thar too.

Unh-hunh. Well. Yu're probly right. His gnarled hand digs deep into his beard, scratching at the roots. He looks around at the others. *Sumbody* should likely oughter go down thar.

The men of the gang, half-circling around, stare at him sullenly in the darkness. There is a lengthy silence, broken only by the train engine letting off a bit of steam deep in the earth. Awright, he says finally. But shares accordin. There's some grumbling, but Belle says: Shore. Heck. Thet's fair.

As he steps the mare toward the mine shaft, however, she rears and balks, forcing him to dismount (better to go in on foot any-way, he reasons, allows for a better chance of ducking out of its way should it come cannonballing up out of there), then plants her body lengthways in front of the black mouth of the tunnel, blocking his way down. She snorts pleadingly, rubbing her nose against his buckskin shirt, forcing him back. He steadies himself, one arm over her withers, and whispers into her lowered ear, twitching in front of his nose as if trying to flick flies off it: It's awright. Aint nuthin down thar but a ole gully jumper gone off its rails. And anyhow, shoot. Yu know. I aint got no choice.

❖   ❖   ❖

Once, long ago—he remembers this now as he pushes past the distressed mare and steps into the ink-black mine shaft, blindly feeling his way and as though possessed by some unspoken obligement he does not even recognize—he won a woman in a game of stud poker, one of the sort Belle was singing about earlier. She was, as they said about such women, a nymph of the prairie who had killed a lot of men by charming them to death, so there was a price on her head and bounty hunters were after her. In fact he was himself a bounty hunter at that time, so what in effect he had won was a hundred dollars. His problem was hauling her up to the next fort and cashing her in before rival bounty hunters got to her, so instead of killing her straight off and having to drag her dead weight around, he figured that it was better to keep her on the hoof until he could safely collect. He figured wrong. Should have known better, he was not ignorant of her reputation, but he was young then, and reckless (as if he'd grown any wiser: look where he is now), and untutored in the witching ways of professional prairie nymphs. It was said that she cast her necromantic spells through some ancient member-rubbing metaphysic, so as precaution he strapped a holster betwixt his legs and pulled on an extra pair of pants backwards, then gagged her and tied her hands behind her back. Of course that meant he had to feed and clean her, which tasks led him to the discovery that there were other sorcerous parts of her, and not least her eyes, which never ceased to fix their gaze upon him, a savage gaze, for she was of mixed breed, yet a gaze of such seeming purity and natural goodness that eventually it was all that he could see and he was in her power and she was unbound and practicing her murderous skills upon him. The days that followed blurred into a ceaseless present and, as he felt his life essence draining out of him, he lost all sense of time. And place: even the landscape seemed to change, acquiring a roseate glow, which glow in the end was all that he could see, the intensity of his pleasure, which was also pain, dissolving the world's salients, dips, and bends into a single throbbing rubescent surface that encircled him much as does now this tunnel down which he gropes, itself now also red and pulsing, though that pounding pulse may only be his own, as it no doubt was then, and the redness an illusion cast upon his eyes by the absolute blackness of the mine. Or are now and then the true illusions and is he still in fact ensorcelled, this powerless sinking into the bowels of the earth the nymph's wry theatrical farewell? Perhaps, and yet he seems to recall a sequel, in which, somehow, through force of youthful will, he escaped her dark enchantment and, though almost too weak to stand, subdued and bound her up once more and blindfolded her as well and sought out in the town wherein he soon found himself a preacher who might break the spell. Well, said the preacher, looking her over with his tired yellow eyes, we could tote her down to the river'n try baptizin her. Yu reckon, revrend? Seems a mite tame. The way I baptize em, son, said the preacher with a thin black smile, it either takes or we bury em. So he left her with him and went to the saloon across the way to recover some of his natural vitality. There some men joined him and affably offered to let him buy them a drink and asked him about the light-o'-love he'd towed in, trussed up like a mountain cat set for a skinning, and he freely told them about her, as they were unarmed and lacked ambition beyond the whiskey remaining in the bottle. So yu turned her over t'thet thar ranter whut runs the gospel-mill crost the street? I done so. He figgered he could unwitch her with a theologic river-duckin. Well, pard, I think yu jest lost yerself a hunderd bucks. Thet feller might be a aymen-snortin pulpit banger on Sundays but rest a the time they aint a more robustious hardshelled bounty hunter in the Terrortory. He sat there taking in these ungratifying tidings, feeling his juices starting to churn once more but unable as yet to set his limbs in adequate motion. Tell me then, he said. Whut day's t'day? Dunno, but it aint Sunday lest thet gospel shark sez it is. So, though putting one leg in front of the other still required considerable effort, he took his rifle and went looking for the preacher and found him naked and sucked down to skin and bone and floating face-down in the river. Never saw the prairie nymph again but he's never been certain that he is shut of her, for she left him full of doubts about the world he walks and about himself and what is real and what is of her conjuring.

The train coughs suddenly, quite nearby, startling him, and he presses back against the glowing tunnel wall, but only silence follows. As, cautiously, he edges forward again, it occurs to him (the red walls remind him so: yes, they are no illusion) that his fears of its roaring out and running him down have been for naught, for of course the train has ducked down here cowcatcher first and cannot turn around, that red glow being provided by its caboose lantern. Which, as he rounds a falling bend, he sees, rocking faintly to and fro from the heaving tremors of the trapped engine down at the other end. It cowers there, nose buried in the narrowing tunnel like a whipped puppy trying to hide in a boot.

Well well, he says. Whut deepot's this?

The train lets off an explosive burst of steam and sets its whistle shrieking, its bells clanging, but it's all empty bravado.

He waits for it to cool down and then he says: They aint no way outa here, y'know, cept backin out tailfirst through the hole yu come in. It's all uphill, yu caint git up no speed, and they's a passel a bodaciously wicked desperadoes up thar jest itchin t'take yu apart rivet by rivet when yu come crawlin out. So I reckon the best thing fer yu t'do is give up yer goods right here and go peaceful.

There's another whistle howl and blast of steam and a rattling of the couplings, the caboose lantern bouncing wildly on its hook at the parlor end and sending shadows leaping about the hellish tunnel, but the train knows well it's beat. A final rackety spasm shudders its length, and then the cars slump forward in defeat, knocking dolefully up against one another, and the caboose lantern ceases to sway and hangs limply in dimmed despond.

I'll see to it they dont hurt yu none, he says, and the train, in abject surrender, sighs grandly and commences to spill out its contents. When it has wholly emptied itself, he leads it, its steel drivers and wheels groaning self-pityingly, back up out of the mine shaft. He feels he has been down here for weeks, but it has probably not been so long, though he does emerge into midday sunlight, there to find his gang still mounted and waiting for him as he left them, the black mare foremost, greeting him at the entranceway with an eager whinny and a nuzzle of his chest. Yu kin let the train go, boys, he announces. We aint got no more use of it. It's dumped all its freight down below. Go hep yerself!

Yippee! the men shout, and leap out of their saddles, and, as soon as the train, chugging gloomily, has backed out of the way, they go charging off into the mine, firing their pistols and racing one another for first pick among the goods. He can hear their clattering bootsteps echoing up out of the pitch-black tunnel, the occasional ricocheting shot, their curses as they bounce off the walls and each other and tumble down the shaft. Still sitting on her horse above him—in the sun, her golden palomino has a soiled and scurfy aspect, more the color of day-old cowpatties—the bandit queen takes her mask off and says: I got some news fer yu, kid.

Before she can deliver it, though, they are interrupted by a terrific explosion in the depths of the mine and the tunnel mouth spews forth a macabre and filthy rain. He turns in rage and fires his rifle futilely at the escaping train, showing now only its red-tipped caboose, wagging tauntingly in the sun-bleached distance. He leaps astride his mare, prepared to give chase, but Belle restrains him.

Whoa, cowboy, she says, grabbing the reins. Let it go. We didnt need thet gang no more anyhow. They've ketched the real hoss thief. Yu been pardoned. Yu're a free man. He rests back in the saddle, taking in this unexpected news. Free. The sound of it soughs through him like a freshening wind. He stretches, and the land seems to stretch out around him. In the distance, above where the judas train disappeared, a lonely hawk wheels like a summons. It's time, it spells out upon the slate-blue sky in graceful loops and swirls, to leave this town behind. Even as a badman on the loose he has been held captive by it, but no longer. He strips off his mask and squints off toward the spreading horizon, looking for something out there on the rim to aim at before it all recedes out of sight. Yu kin go back t'bein sheriff agin, darlin. Me'n yu, we kin clean up thet disreptile town.

I dont much cotton to the sheriffin line, mam. Reckon I'll be hittin the trail. The chanteuse, for that's what she is once more, looks sorrowed by the news but not surprised; it's who he is, after all. So who'd they say done it?

Well yu wont hardly believe it. It's the schoolmarm. She come ridin inta town on it, bold as brass.

Whut? But I give her thet hoss.

Dont matter none how she come by it. She wuz settin it and thet wuz fault enuf. They clapped her sanctimonious fanny smack in the calaboose, no questions ast nor answered, thet's all she wrote. They're hangin her tomorra at high noon and good riddance.

The hawk has left the sky, that slate wiped blank. The horizon has shrunk toward him some, but whether to urge or thwart his departure is not clear, and the wind has died, if it was ever blowing. His mare snorts impatiently, paws the ground. He strokes her neck. Did yu say thet sheriff's job wuz open?

I thought yu wuz boltin off inta the sunset.

Dont seem t'be thet time a day. Anyhow, I reckon I caint go jest yet.

Now yu're talkin, sweetie. I knowed yu couldnt leave me. C'mon! I still got thet silk'n velvet gown with all them buttons and almost nuthin spilt on it. Lets git goin!

Y'know, what gits me, says the chanteuse, gazing down upon the town, laid out below in parallel lines as though to lend conviction that it is somewhere, is how sad it is, settin thar like a speck in the middle a nuthin. And how grand.

Peculiar, more like, he says. They have arrived at a bluff overlooking the town, a prominence he had not noticed before. Dont see nobody movin down thar.

Thet's jest cuzza us bein up so high.

We aint so high I caint read the saloon sign nor see the curtain hangin in yer winder.

And aint it a purty sight! She reaches over and clasps his buckskinned thigh. He can also see the gallows, which, like the rest of the town, is presently unoccupied, a relief to him because he was afraid a day might have passed in their coming here and he might be too late. Unless it's already the day after. Caint wait t'git back inta my own satin sheets. She sighs, giving his leg an eager squeeze. It aint in my maidenly nature t'be livin rough.

Belle, he says, they's sumthin I gotta talk t'yu about.

Only one thing though, darlin: I aint sharin my bed with thet damned hoss.

Well thet's jest it. Yu wont hafta do.

Course not. But lookie thar!

Down below, the streets are now full of diminutive figures running about in an aimless frenzy like a colony of ants whose nest has been poked. They scramble in and out of buildings, dash across streets, fall off rooftops and out of windows, whirl, roll, and tumble, and though it all happens in a heavy midday silence, he realizes that they must be shooting at each other. Yes, he can see flashes now, puffs of smoke. And then the sound does reach them: a series of stuttery little pops like strings of firecrackers going off.

I'd say thet's a town desprit fer a sheriff, the chanteuse remarks. I jest hope they aint shot the parson.

The dead are dragged away or carried off by buzzards and the figures vanish, though the pops continue for a time before also dying away. Then the buildings shift about like wagers on a faro table, the bank moving over to where the saloon was, the saloon replacing the church now sliding into the center next to the stables, the claims office and the jailhouse changing places either side of the general store, and so on, until the entire town layout has been reset. The streets are empty and silence reigns as before. He feels he has just witnessed something vital but he does not know what it is, nor can he fix his mind wholly upon it, so assailed is it by dire apprehensions about a certain person and the danger she is in. Dont fret about no parson, Belle, he says. I aint stayin. They's sumthin I gotta attend to. And then I'll be movin on.

Suddenly the figures reappear in the streets below, scampering, rolling, and falling about as before, scribbling their miserable fates on the town's dusty tablet, and a moment later the stutter of pops resumes, tattooing the desert air. He is not certain how he will manage what he has to do, but the simplest and boldest thing would be just to ride down there, pick her up, put her on his horse, and ride away, and he supposes it's what he'll do, or try to do. If she'll allow him. There's a fierce principled streak in her that can get in the way of amiable intentions. He envisions the struggle, and his lips twitch involuntarily into a half smile. Whut's she got that I aint got twice of? asks the chanteuse flatly, her voice hardening.

He presses his lips together, feeling like someone's just peeked at his hand in a poker showdown. It aint thet. The little figures below withdraw and the streets are cleared and the buildings slide about once more as though trying to solve some puzzle. It's jest she aint no hoss thief, and I caint let her die fer thet.

Hmmph, says Belle in the silence that returns. Her tasseled sombrero has been tipped back onto her shoulders and her orange hair is blazing in the sun like her whole head's on fire. Thet harpy is homely as a fencepost and friendly as a dead cat and she aint even bowlaigged enuf t'set a hoss proper. Ifn it wuz me they wuz hangin, yu'da been long gone, wouldnt yu, handsome?

She's differnt, Belle. He remembers her as he first saw her, framed in the schoolhouse window, her dark hair coiled into a tight bun, so very pale and beautiful and staring out at him as if to instruct him by gaze alone on the ways of the universe and the means for quelling the spirits of evil in the human heart. She's kindly and reefined and pure as a angel. She caint think a wicked thought.

Damn her eyes. She's a prissy bitch with a cob stuck purely up her reefined angel ass. I caint stand the proud uppish way she talks, struttin her book larnin. Whut's sumbody like her doin out here anyhow? The chanteuse pauses to collect her breath, which is coming in short furious gasps. There is a look on her face that reminds him of his mustang just before he shot him. Well jest dont yu fergit, cowboy. Yu made a promise.

He sighs. This is not turning out as he'd imagined it. He'd even thought that Belle might help him. Aint no witnesses t'thet promise, Belle.

No? How many folks yu reckon is down thar?

They are dashing about through the streets again in their hats and batwing chaps, shooting at each other, diving for cover, appearing on the tops of things only to fall off them, the buzzards as usual hovering shaggily above like bald black-jacketed croupiers, surveying the action, waiting to gather in the winnings. The thin *puppety-pop* code of distant gunfire rises as the agitation diminishes and the streets empty out, and then it dies, too. I dunno, he says, as the little buildings rearrange themselves around the gallows again. A goodly number, I spose. They dont stand still long enuf t'count.

Well however many, sweetiepie, thet's how many witnesses I got.

The streets of the town below are empty and silent as before and hotly burnished by the noonday sun. Into them on a coal-black horse now rides a lone figure all outfitted in black with silver spurs and six-shooters and a gold ring in one ear. It is he. A man on a mission. The chanteuse has left him in anger and disgust, or seems to have done, nothing he could do about that, and here he is. From under the broad brim of his slouch hat he warily watches, feeling watched, the windows and rooftops, the corners of things. Expecting trouble. The mare seems edgy too, rolling her head fretfully, biting at the bit. Well, she's an outlaw horse, has likely never set hoof in this town before except on illegal business; she probably has good reason for unease.

In the center of town across from the saloon, a potbellied mestizo with a missing ear and a tall squint-eyed man with droopy handlebars and a bald head tattooed with hair are testing the trapdoor of the gallows, using a noosed goat, not by the appearance of it for the first time. Yo, sheriff! the man with the tattooed hair calls out, dragging the goat into position. Howzit hangin?

He nods at them and watches the limp goggle-eyed goat drop, then walks the mare cautiously over to the jailhouse. So he's the sheriff again. Yes, he's wearing his silver badge once more, the one with the hole in it. That explains the sharp tug in the breast he's felt since turning his back on the inviting horizon and riding back to town again. Shines out on his black shirt in a way it never did before.

There's a poster outside the jailhouse door announcing the high noon hanging on the morrow, with a portrait of the schoolmarm staring sternly out at all who would dare stare back. He is shaken by the intensity of her gaze, and the pure gentle innocence of it, and the rectitude, and he knows he is lost to it.

He hitches the mare to the rail there, and though she is skittish and backs away, her eyes rolling, tugging at her tether, he needs her for what he must next do. He unhooks his rifle from the saddle horn. I'll jest be a minnit and then we'll hightail it outa here, he says softly, stroking her sweaty neck to calm her, and he enters the jailhouse ready for whatever happens.

But the jailhouse is empty, nobody in there except an old codger with an eyepatch, slumped in the wooden swivel chair, wearing a deputy's badge on his raggedy red undershirt. There is a thick gully of scar running through his gray beard, down which a trickle of tobacco juice dribbles, and his lone eye is red with drink. Hlo, shreriff, he drawls, trying to stand. Glad yu're back. Yu're jest in time t'hang thet rapscallious hoss thief yerself. He chortles, then falls back into the swivel chair, takes a swig from a whiskey bottle, belches, offers it out. Yer health, sheriff!

Whar is she? he says.

The prizner? They tuck her over t'the saloon t'shuck her weeds offn her'n scrub her down afore her hangin.

The saloon?

Yup, well they got soap'n water over thar and plentya hep in spiffyin her up. The boys wuz plannin t'rub her down good with goose grease'n skunk oil after, polish her up right properlike. He's already at the door and there's a pounding in his temples that's worse than snakebite. Hey, hole up, sheriff! Ain't thet a outlaw hoss out thar?

Mebbe. I'll check into it. Yu stay here'n keep yer workin eye on thet whuskey bottle.

I aim to.

The mare is wild-eyed and frothing, rearing against her hitching rope, so he lets her go. Stay outa sight, he whispers to her as he unties her. This wont take long. I'll whistle yu when we're set t'bust out. The horse hesitates, pawing the ground, whinnying softly, but he slaps her haunches affectionately, and, glancing back over her shoulder at him, she slips away into the shadows behind the jailhouse.

The object of his quest is not in the saloon either. It's quiet in there, four men playing cards, a couple more at the bar, a puddle of water in the middle of the floor where a bucket of soapy water stands, a lacy black thing ripped up and hung over its lip. The men at the bar are laughing and pointing at the bucket or else at the wet long-handled grooming brush beside it. Thet goddam humpback! one of them says, hooting.

Hlo, sheriff, grins the bartender, a dark sleepy-eyed man of mixed breed with half a nose. Welcum back. Whut's yer pizen?

An argument breaks out at the card table, the air fills with the slither of steel flashing free of leather, shots ring out, and a tall skinny man with spidery hair loses most of his jaw and all else besides, slamming against the wall with the impact before sliding in a bloody heap to the floor. Looks like they's a chair open fer yu, sheriff, says the thin little bespectacled man who shot him, tucking his smoking derringer back inside his black broadcloth coat. Set yer butt down and study the devil's prayerbook a spell.

I aint a sportin man. Whut's happened t'the prizner?

Yu mean thet dastardly hoss thief? Haw. Caint say. He aims a brown slather of juice at a brass spittoon, and it crashes there, making the spittoon rattle on its round bottom like a gambling top. She might could be over t'doc's fer a purjin so's t'git her cleaned up inside as smart as out, though after her warshin in here, I misdoubt she needs it.

The others snort and hoot at this. Naw, I think doc musta aweady seed her, declares the barkeep, a toothpick stabbed into a gap between his tobacco-stained teeth. He was in here shortly sniffin his finger.

Probly then, laughs another, they tuck her up t'the schoolhouse fer a paddlin.

Whut's thet got t'do with bein a hoss thief?

Nuthin. It's jest fer fun. Give the jade summa her own back. And they all whoop again and slap the bar and table.

He pushes out through the swinging doors, his blood pounding in his ears and eyes. Can't recollect where the doctor lives, if he ever knew, so he heads for the schoolhouse. On his way over, he hears a banging noise coming from a workshop back of the feed store. It's a lanky hairy-faced carpenter knocking out a pine coffin. Howdy, sheriff, he says, lifting the coffin up on its foot. Jest gittin ready t'cut the lid. Inside, on the bottom, there is a crude line drawing of a stretched-out human figure, no doubt done by tracing around a person lying there. One of the faces from the hanging posters has been cut out and pasted in the outline of the head, and nails have been driven in where the nipples would be. The arms go only to the elbows (probably her hands were folded between the nails), but the legs are there in all their forked entirety. I reckon it should oughter fit her perfect. Whuddayu think?

I think yu should oughter burn it.

The schoolhouse is not where he remembered it either. Instead, he comes on a general dry goods and hardware store in that proximate neighborhood and he stops in to ask if she's been seen about.

Sheriff! Whar yu been? cries the merchant, a round bandy-legged fellow with a black toupee and his nose pushed into his red face. They's been a reglar plague a hell-raisin bandits pilin through here since yu been gone! Jest lookit whut they done t'my store! Shot up my winders, killt my staff, stole summa my finest goods, 'n splattered blood'n hossshit on all the rest! Yu gotta do sumthin about this! Whut's a sheriff fer ifn honest folk caint git pertection!

Thet's a question I aint got a clear answer to, he says, staring coldly into the fat merchant's beady eyes. Right now I'm tryin t'locate a missin prizner.

Whut, yu mean thet ornery no-account barebutt picaroon? She aint missin. Yer boys wuz by here a time ago with her, plain cleaned me outa hosswhips'n ax handles; she wuz in fer a grand time. I think they wuz makin fer the stables. Yu know. Scene a the crime. He turns to leave, but the merchant has a grip on his elbow and a salacious grin on his round red face. I gotta tell yu, sheriff, I seen sumthin when they brung her by I aint never seed before. He glances over his shoulder with one eye, the other winking, and leans toward him, his cold fermented breath ripe with the stink of rot and mildew. She wuz—huh! yu know, he snickers softly in his ear. She wuz *cryin*!

He tears free from the merchant's greasy grip and strides out the door onto the wooden porch, his spurs ringing in the midday hush. He pauses there to stare out upon the dusty town. No sign of them. They could be anywhere. There's a dim shadowy movement over in the blacksmith's shed, but that's probably his horse pacing about. He should just go back to the jailhouse and wait for them. But then the white church steeple beckons him. She gave him a Bible once, he recalls. They'll have to take her there sooner or later if she wants to go, and she surely will. There's probably a law about it.

❖   ❖   ❖

He is met inside the church doors by the parson, or *a* parson, standing in a black frock coat behind a wooden table with a Bible on it, a pair of ivory dice (REPENT, says a tented card beside them, AFORE YU CRAP OUT!), a pistol, and a collection plate. Howdo, sheriff, he says, touching the brim of his stovepipe hat. He's a tall ugly gold-toothed man with wild greasy hair snaking about under the hat and a drunkard's lumpy nose, on the end of which a pair of wire-rimmed spectacles is perched like two pans of a gold-dust balance. Welcum t'the house a the awmighty. Yu're jest in time fer evenin prayers!

I aint here fer prayin. I'm lookin fer a missin prizner.

Y'mean thet jezebel hoss thief? She gone missin? A leather flap behind the parson blocks his view, but he can hear the churchgoers carrying on inside, hooting and hollering in the pietistical way. Well she's probly in thar, ever other sinner is.

Thanks, revrend, he says, and heads on in, but the parson grabs him by the elbow. The pistol is cocked and pointed at his ear. Whoa thar, brother. I caint let yu go in without payin.

I tole yu, I aint here fer the preachin, I'm on sheriffin bizness.

Dont matter. Yu gotta put sumthin in the collection plate or I caint let yu by.

I aint got no money, he says firmly, staring down the gun barrel. And I'm goin in thar.

Dont hafta be money, says the parson, keeping the pistol pointed at his head but letting go of his elbow to tug at his reversed collar so as to give his Adam's apple more room to bob. Them sporty boots'll do.

No. Gonna need them boots. If he just walked on in, would the preacher shoot him in the back? He might.

Well how about thet thar beaded black-haired scalp then?

He hesitates. He doesn't know why he wears it. For good luck, maybe. Like a rabbit's paw. But he's not superstitious. And it doesn't even smell all that good. Awright, he says, and he cuts it off his gunbelt with his bowie knife and tosses it in the collection plate, where it twists and writhes for a moment before curling up like a dead beetle.

Now I'll roll yu fer them boots, ifn yu're of a mind fer it, grins the parson goldenly, picking up the dice and rattling them about in his grimy knob-knuckled hand, but he pushes on past him under the flap into the little one-room church, the preacher calling out behind him: I'm sorely beseechin the good Lawd thet yu localize thet snotnose gallows bird, sheriff! Dont wanta lose her at the last minnit and set all hell t'grievin!

Veiled gas lamps hang from blackened beams in the plank-walled room, the air hazy with smoke and smelling of stale unwashed bodies and the nauseous vapors of the rotgut whiskey—drunk, undrunk, and regurgitated—being served like communion from boards set on pew backs. Hanging in the thick smoke like audible baubles are the ritual sounds of ringing spittoons, dice raining upon craps tables, the clink of money, soft slap of cards, the ratcheting and ping of fortune wheels and slot machines, the *click click click* of the roulette ball, and, amid the zealous cries of the high rollers, oaths are being sworn and glasses smashed and pistols fired off with a kind of emotional abandon. Are yu all down, gentamin? someone hollers, and another cries out: Gawd-awmighty, smack me easy! Somewhere in the church, behind all the smoke and noise, he can hear the saloon chanteuse singing about a magical hero with a three-foot johnnie, now hung and gone to glory, her voice half smothered by the thick atmosphere. Sweat-stained hats hang in parade on hooks along the walls under doctrinal pronouncements regarding spitting and fair dealing, rows of decapitated animal heads, dusty silvered mirrors which reflect nothing, and religious paintings of dead bandits and unclothed ladies in worshipful positions, but the only sign anywhere of the one he's looking for is one of the posters announcing tomorrow's hanging nailed up over a faro table, the portrait obscenely altered. BUCK THE TIGER! it says, and a crude drawing shows where and how to do so.

He turns a corner (there is a corner, the room is getting complicated) and comes upon a craps table with strange little misshapen dice, more like real knucklebones, which they probably are. Set down, sheriff, and shake an elbow, says the scrubby skew-jawed fellow in dun-colored rags and bandanna headband who is working the table, a swarthy and disreputable wretch who is vaguely familiar. His broken arm is in a rawhide sling, its hand fingerless, and there's a fresh red weal across his rough cheeks, the sort of cut made by a horsewhip. Here, he can no longer hear the chanteuse; instead, at the back by the big wheel of fortune, there is a choral rhythmic rise and fall of drunken whoops, so it's likely she's back there somewhere. Not someone he cares to see just now. Go ahaid'n roll em, sheriff, says the wampus-jawed scrub, wagging the stump at the end of his broken arm. Them sad tats is mine. Wuz.

Aint got no stake. But dont I know yu from sumwhars? With his good hand, the wretch flashes a bent and rusty deputy's badge, hidden away in his filthy rags. Whut? Yu my deppity?

Useter be. But I lost my poke'n then some in thet wicked brace over by the big wheel. I hafta work fer this clip crib now.

Whar's the prizner then?

Well we lost her too.

Lost her—?

T'thet hardass double-dealin shark over thar, the dodrabbid burglar whut operates this skin store. He's the one whut give me this extry elbow and my own bones t'flop when I opened my big mouth after ketchin him with a holdout up his sleeve. He sees him now, enthroned behind a blackjack table under a glowing gas lamp, over by the wheel of fortune, an immense bald and beardless man in a white suit and ruffled shirt with blue string tie and golden studs, wearing blue-tinted spectacles smack up against his eyes. He sits as still and pale as stone, nothing moving except his little fat fingers, deftly flicking out the cards. The rhythmic whooping is coming from there and may be in response to the cards being dealt. The motherless asshole tuck us fer all we had, sheriff. Got the prizner in the bargain.

Yu done wrong. She warnt a stake.

I know it.

Whut's he done with her?

Well. His ex-deputy hesitates. It aint nice. He glances uneasily over his shoulder. Best go on over thar'n see fer yerself.

There's an icy chill on his heart and a burning rage at the same time and he feels like he might go crazy with the sudden antipodal violence of his feelings, but he bites down hard and collects himself and sets his hat square over his brow and drops his hands flat to his sides and straightens up his back and lowers his head and, with measured strides, makes his way over toward the glowing fat man at the blackjack table. The room seems to have spread out somewhat or to be spreading out as he proceeds, and there are new turns and corners he must bear around, sudden congestions of loud drunken gamblers he must thread his way through, and sometimes the blackjack dealer seems further away than when he first set out, but he presses on, learning to follow not his eyes but his ears (those whoops and hollers), and so is drawn in time into the crowd of men around the blackjack table. What is provoking their rhythmic hoots, he sees when he gets there, is the sight of the schoolmarm stretched out upon the slowly spinning wheel of fortune, her black skirts falling past her knees each time she's upside down. He tries not to watch this but is himself somewhat mesmerized by the rhythmic rising and falling, revealing and concealing, of the schoolmarm's dazzling white knees, the spell broken only when he realizes that she is gazing directly at him as she rotates with a look compounded of fury, humiliation, and anguished appeal. It is a gaze most riveting when she is upside down and the whoops are loudest, her eyes then darkly underscored by eyebrows as if bagged with grief, her nose with its flared nostrils fiercely horning her brow between them, the exposed knees above not unlike a bitter thought, and a reproach.

He steps forward, not knowing what he will do, but before he can reach the table, a tall bald man with tattooed hair pushes everyone aside and, tossing down a buckskin purse, seats himself before it. Dole me some paint thar, yu chiselin jackleg! he bellows with drunken bravado, twirling the waxed ends of his handlebar mustache. He's seen him before, testing out the gallows, except that since then he's acquired a wooden leg. His partner, the one-eared mestizo, now wearing a bear claw in his nose and an erect feather in a headband, hovers nearby with his pants gaped open under his overhanging belly. I'm aimin t'win summa thet gyratin pussy fer my bud'n me, and I dont wanta ketch yu spikin, stackin, trimmin, rimplin, nickin, nor ginnyin up in no manner them books, dont wanta see no shiners, cold decks, coolers, nor holdouts, nor witness no great miracles a extry cards or a excess a greased bullets. Yu hear? So now rumble the flats, yu ole grifter, and cut me a kiss.

The dealer, holding the deck of cards in his soft smooth bejeweled hands as a sage might clasp a prayerbook, has sat listening to all this bluster with serene indifference, his hairless head settled upon his layered folds of chin like a creamy mound of milk curd, eyes hidden behind the sky-blue spectacles, which seem almost pasted to them. The tinted spectacles, he knows, are for reading the backs of doped cards, the polished rings for mirroring the deal, a pricking poker ring no doubt among them, and the man's sleeves and linen vest are bulked and squared by the mechanical holdout devices concealed within. When, so minimally one can almost not see the movement, he shuffles, cuts, and deals, he seems to use at least three different decks, crosscutting a pair of them, and the deal is from the bottom of the only deck in view at any one time, or at least not from the top.

The squint-eyed man with the tattooed hair rises up and kicks his chair back with his wooden leg. I jest come unanimously to the conclusion yu been cheatin, he shouts, as the dealer calmly slides the man's leather purse into his heap of winnings, then takes up the deck to reshuffle it, so smoothly that the deck seems like a small restless creature trapped between his soft pale hands. Behind him, the schoolmarm, bound to the fortune wheel, grimly turns and turns, though now, with the bald man on his feet, or foot, the rhythmic whooping dies away.

Easy, podnuh, whispers the one-eared mestizo, his hand inside his pants. He spits over his shoulder, away from the dealer. He's awmighty fast, thet sharper. Dont try him. It aint judicious.

Shet up, yu yellabellied cyclops,'n gimme room! the bald man roars. He stands there before the bespectacled dealer, legs apart and leaning on his pegleg, shoulders tensed, elbows out, hands hovering an inch from his gunbutts. I'm callin yer bluff, yu flim-flammin cartload a hossshit!

A hole opens up explosively in the bald man's chest like a post has been driven through it, kicking him back into the crowd, the dealer having calmly drawn, fired, and reholstered without even interrupting his steady two-handed shuffle of the cards. He sets the deck down and spreads his plump palms to either side as though to say: Any other sucker here care to try his luck?

He makes certain his sheriff's badge is in plain view, tugs at the brim of his hat, hitches his gunbelt, and steps into the well-lit space just abruptly vacated by the peglegged man with the tattooed hair. He picks up the fallen chair, watching the dealer closely, and sets it down in front of the blackjack table but remains standing. I'm askin yu t'return me back my prizner, he says quietly. He has a hunch about the dealer now, something he grows more convinced of the longer he stands there studying him. She warnt a legal bet. Yu knowed thet. I may hafta close this entaprize down.

His weedy ex-deputy with the busted arm leans close to the dealer, who seems, though his thick lips do not move, to whisper something in his crumpled ear. He sez he dont spect thet'll happen, says the ex-deputy out the side of his mouth. Behind the mountainous fat man, the revolving schoolmarm's white knees rise into view like a pair of expressionless stocking-capped puppets, then fall into curtained obscurity, over and over, but he steels himself to pay them no heed, and to ignore as well her burning gaze, for now he must think purely on one thing and one thing only. He sez ifn yu want back thet renegade hoss thief, yu should oughter set yerself down'n play him a hand fer her.

Caint. Aint got no poke. Yes, he's sure of it now. It's why he sits so still. Listening. To everything. His ears thumbing the least sound the way his pink-tipped sandpapered fingers caress the cards. Behind those blue spectacles, the man is blind.

Well whut about yer boots? suggests the ex-deputy. Or yer weepons? He shakes his head. The ex-deputy whispers something in the fat man's ear, then tips his own ear close to attend to the reply. Well awright, he sez. Yer life then, he sez. Yer'n fer her'n.

Hunh. Shore, he shrugs, and sits down on the edge of the chair to get his voice into the right position. Aint wuth a plug nickel nohow. A flicker of amusement seems to cross the fat man's face, the reawakened cards fluttering between his hands like a caged titmouse, or a feeding hummingbird. He removes his spurs so they will not betray him, and then, leaving his voice behind, rises silently from the chair to slip around behind the dealer. Reglar five-card stud, his voice says. Face up. Dont want nuthin hid. The dealer offers the deck toward the chair. No cut, mister. Jest dole em out. The room has fallen deadly silent as he circles round, nothing to be heard but the creaking and ticking of the wheel of fortune, all murmurs stilled, which may be perplexing the fat man, though he gives no sign of it. With barely a visible movement, he deals the empty chair a jack and himself a king. I reckon yu're tryin t'tell me sumthin, his voice says from the chair, keeping up the patter to cover his movements. Something an old deerhunter once taught him as a way of confusing his prey. It was a simple trick and so natural that, once he learned it, he was amazed he had not always known how to do it. But a pair a these here young blades'll beat a sucked-out ole bulldog any day, his voice adds cockily when a second jack falls, a second king of course immediately following on. Uh-oh, says his voice. Damn my luck. Pears I'll require a third one a them dandies jest t'stay in this shootout. Which he gets, it in turn topped by a third king. He is behind the dealer now, gazing down upon his bubbly mound of glowing pate. Well would yu lookit thet, says his voice, as the fourth jack is turned up. I reckon now, barrin miracles, the prizner's mine. Stealthily, as the fourth king falls, he unsheathes his bowie knife. The dealer's head twitches slightly as though he might have heard something out of order and were cocking his ear toward it, so his voice says from the chair: Aint thet sumthin! Four jacks! Four kings! But we aint done yet, podnuh. Yu owe me another card. Yu aint doled out but four. The fat man hesitates, tipping slightly toward the voice, then, somewhat impatiently, flicks out a black queen, which falls like a provocation between the two hands of armed men. Well ifn thet dont beat all, his voice exclaims. How'd

128

thet fifth jack git in thar? The dealer starts, seems about to reach for his gun or the card, but stays his hand and, after the briefest hesitation, flips over a fifth king. Haw, says the voice. Nuthin but a mizzerbul deuce. Gotcha, ole man! And as the gun comes out and blasts the chair away, he buries the blade deep in the dealer's throat, slicing from side to side through the thick piled-up flesh like stirring up a bucket of lard.

The man does not fall over but continues to sit there in his rotundity as before, his head slumping forward slightly as though in disappointment, his blue spectacles skidding down his nose away from the puckery dimples where eyes once were. His gun hand twitches off another shot, shattering an overhead lamp and sending everyone diving for cover, then turns up its palm and lets the pistol slip away like a discard. A white fatty ooze leaks from the slit throat, slowly turning pink. He wipes his blade on the shoulders of the man's white linen suit, triggering a mechanical holdout mechanism that sends a few aces flying out his sleeves, and then he carefully resheathes it, eyeing the others all the while as they pick themselves up and study this new circumstance. He's not sure how they will take it or just who this dealer was to them, so to distract them from any troublous thoughts they may be having, he says: Looks like them winnins is up fer grabs, gentamin.

That sets off the usual crazed melee, and while they are going at it he arrests the wheel of fortune to free the schoolmarm. When he releases her wrists, he half expects her to slap his face again, but instead she faints and collapses over his shoulder, her hands loosely whacking him behind, so that he has to unbind her hips and ankles with the full weight of her upon him. It is getting ugly in the churchroom, guns and knives are out and fists and bottles are flying, so he quickly sidles out of there, toting her beam-high over his shoulder like a saddlebag, the room conveniently shrinking toward the exit to hasten his passage. At the door, before darting out into the night, he glances back over his free shoulder at the mayhem within (this is his town and for all he knows the only people he has ever had and he is about to leave them now forever) and sees through the haze the dead dealer, still slumped there under the glowing lamp like an ancient melancholic ruin, his hairless blue-bespectacled head slowly sinking away into his oozing throat.

✧   ✧   ✧

He strides, under a tapestry of faintly pulsing stars, through the desolate town, whistling softly for his horse, one hand gripping a lax tender thigh, the other clasped behind her skirted knees. He assumes the church will not long contain the turmoil within, but his hopes of getting out of here quickly are fading. He headed first for the blacksmith's shed where last he spied the black mare, but the shed was not where he remembered it to be; finding the jailhouse with the gallows out front instead, he made next for the stables but wound up again at the jail. She was getting heavy, so he thought to hide her in her schoolhouse until he could locate the mare or some other horse or pair of horses, but he has come once more to the gallows and the jailhouse, or they have come to him. He stands there by the hanging place in the hushed darkness, whistling softly, frustration welling up in his breast (where is that damned horse?), trying to get his bearings, his cheek pressed against a flexuous hip, his arms hugging her legs as if they were the one sure thing he might still hold on to. Tacked up on the scaffold is one of the posters announcing the schoolmarm's high-noon hanging on the morrow, though in the dim starlight her portrait's fierce severity seems to have mellowed, as though surrendering to whatever fate awaits her. He is determined she will not hang—if asked why he has come here, he would now say this was why—and it is as if the portrait recognizes that and so looks out upon him more with hope than outrage; but just how he is to accomplish her rescue is not yet clear to him, which may account for the gentle perplexity he also seems to read upon the portrait's face, its gaze beseeching, its lips slightly parted as though to ask a question, or receive a kiss. Of farewell? He feels a pricking in the corners of his eyes and water forms there, which he supposes must be tears. He must not fail her. He turns his head away from that dread instrument with its noosed rope hanging high against the night, and this loner, this aloof and restless gunslinger, footloose, free, beholden to no one and no thing, presses his lips reverently against the softness there upon his shoulder, gazing past the sweet black hillock of her haunch at the field of throbbing stars in the moonless sky beyond and thinking: I am wholly lost and am not who I thought I was.

He is about to set off on another search for horse or cover when he hears the church letting out behind him and the men pouring clamorously into the street. There's no time; they seem to be approaching rapidly from all directions, hollering out their rapturous oaths and maledictions and firing off their weapons. He jogs heavily across the street, feeling pursued now, the schoolmarm's head bouncing against his back (the beseeching gaze, parted lips: he's not thinking upon these now, though he knows he surely will again), and ducks into the jailhouse, but, encumbered by the burden of her, he cannot throw the bolt before the men of the town come pounding in and push him back.

Yo, sheriff! Lookit whut yu got thar!

Haw! Aint she a gratifyin sight!

Done hit the jackpot, the sheriff did!

They light the lamps and circle about him, filling up the room, raucously admiring the woman slung over his shoulder, reaching out to try to palpate her lifeless parts or poke at them with their greasy gunbarrels. He fends them off as best he can, backing toward the cell door, considering his choices. Probably he has none.

We wuz afeerd we wuz gonna miss out our neck-stretchin party!

Yu done good, sheriff! Yu done right by the lawr!

Now whynt yu go treat yerself to a easeful potation, podnuh, and rest up fer the big day, says a toothless pop-eyed hunchback tented in a voluminous white linen jacket with a deputy's badge pinned upside down to its stained lapel. We'll take keera the prizner fer yu.

No, he says. In former times he would have simply shot his way out of here, tried to; can't do that now. Yu'll leave her be. She aint gonna hang.

Whut—?

I'm lettin her go.

Yu caint do thet, sheriff! Yu aint got the right!

We built thet new gallows jest fer her!

Hadta use up the whole back halfa the feed store fer the wood!

Caint hep thet. She aint the one. I stole thet hoss.

Yu whut—?

The men fall back momentarily, their jovial mien turned dark, while under his hand the schoolmarm's thigh twitches and stiffens as though tweaked awake by his stark confession. Put me down, she demands icily from behind his back, and all the softness seems to go out of her. Immediately, please.

Tarnation, someone mutters, and fires a gob into the cell behind him for exclamatory punctuation. Looks like we'll hafta change the pitcher on all them fuckin posters.

He drops to his knees to set her feet on the floor, watched closely by the surly men crowding round once more, and she straightens up above him, touching his shoulder briefly to brace herself, a touch, though merely expedient, for which he is grateful.

He continues to kneel there for a moment, as if petitioning for mercy, which is perhaps what he's doing, but without another word she turns on her stolid black heels and, hands clasped at her waist, struts away toward the door, the men removing their hats and backing off to let her pass. It is not his wont to break a silence, but faced with the dreadful and endless one to which he is now condemned (which he will confront, when she is gone, with the quiet stoicism that is his nature and by which he's known, and has known himself), he cannot help himself: Yu aint never even thanked me, he calls out.

She turns back at the open door, framed by the velvety black night behind her. There is not much of affection in her gaze, but he is encouraged even by the lack of undue choler. Not ain't, she replies, quietly but firmly. You *have* never thanked me.

No? He is somewhat bewildered but full aware he owes her much, and he stands up and takes his hat off as the others have done. Sorry, mam. But you aint thanked me neither.

She sighs and shakes her head. For what have I to thank you?

Well. Yu know. Fer whut I jest done. Fer savin yer life.

I did not steal that horse. You did what you had to do.

No. He finds it difficult to meet her hard steady gaze, which he believes now to be the color of cast iron, so stares instead at the dark dimplelike beauty mark on her cheek. Thet warnt the reason I done it.

That *was* not the reason that you *did* it.

No, mam.

So what was that reason, pray tell?

I . . . I caint say it.

Cannot say it.

No, mam. Jest caint.

She sighs, and though she glowers still, there is more of tenderness in that sigh than there has been in her before.

Y'know whut? I think the sheriff's got a soft spot fer the marm!
Y'reckon?

She pauses there by the door, watching him for a moment in all
her straight-backed rectitude, and then that stern righteousness
melts away and, haltingly, she comes back into the room, her black
skirts whispering, and stands mildly before him in the lamplight,
tipping her head to catch his wayward glance, as if beseeching him
to look at her, and, with an awful weakness spreading through
him, he does.

Well but does the marm have a soft spot fer the sheriff?

Haw! Ifn she does, I reckon I know whar yu kin find it!

Shet yer trap now! I think he's gonna kiss her!

Whut? I caint believe it!

Nor can he. His eyes are full of this new sight—her softened
brow, the searching gaze, her moist parted lips—brand new, even
unimaginable until this moment, and yet somehow so familiar he
feels he's seen this face turned to him thus yieldingly all his nat-
ural-born life, and he leans toward it, his eyes closing, as if finding
at last what had long been lost.

Thar he goes!

Now we'll hafta hang him shore!

The warmth of her breath has just fallen damply upon his
parched lips when there is a sudden violent explosion that shakes
the whole jailhouse—instinctively he pushes her aside, spins
round, and draws: it is the black mare, wild-eyed and swelled up
to twice her size, who's come crashing in on them, taking out door,
frame, and a portion of the wall, shattering all the windows with
the impact, and sending the men scrambling and tumbling now to
get out of the way of her rampageous hoofs.

Hey! Look out! It's thet outlaw mare! they cry. She's gone loco!

The schoolmarm has fallen to the floor behind him in the open
cell door and is clinging to his legs. He tries whistling to the mare

to calm her but it seems only to enrage her all the more. Up she rises against the ceiling, frothing at the mouth and nostrils flared, and down she comes, crushing all in her path and sending glass and dust and woodchips flying.

Look out!

Halp! I caint see! I think I ketched a splinter in my eye!

She's mashed my laig!

The white-jacketed bent-backed deputy grabs a lasso off a wall peg and with a grunt flings it over the crazed horse's neck, but she rears up and with a single blow stoves his head in with her hoof, spraying them all with blood and brains and leaving nothing on the deputy's busted neck but his toothless lower jaw, hanging there like a melon rind.

Do sumthin, sheriff! Git aholt on thet devil hoss afore she's killt us all!

Shoot the goddam animule! Whuddayu waitin fer?

He is face-to-face now with the foaming red-eyed beast, his back to the empty cell, roped to that place by the schoolmarm's entwining arms. Both his pistols are pointed at the mare's rolling eyeballs, but, for all that she has spoilt his singular moment with the marm, he cannot bring himself to pull the triggers, for he has never had a horse like this one and he does not want with rash haste to lose her. Particularly not now when he might most need her. She snorts and whinnies, shakes her black mane fearsomely, pounds the floor with her hoof, then seems to pump it toward his legs, behind which the schoolmarm is cowering still, peeking out between them. Then up she goes again, her forelegs churning, hind legs stepping forward, her neigh more like a terrifying shriek, and she comes crashing down (the schoolmarm screams), smashing, over and over, at the bars of the cell on either side of him.

It's the marm she's after!

Give her over, sheriff! Dont rile thet savage critter up no worse'n it is!

Now hole up thar, damn yu! he yells at the maddened mare. Yu back off! Yu wanta stomp sumbody, yu pestiferous jughaided scrag, yu stomp me! The horse blows through her nostrils and bangs the floor, and arches her head back so far toward her tail all he can see is her black throat, and lets out a whinny more like a quivering howl. Then she drops her head down between her knees and peers at him beseechingly from under her forelock, scuffing at the floor planks with one hoof. Awright, thet's better. Now git outa here, he says. She swings her head from side to side, her lips curled away from her teeth, her damp gaze now more aggrieved than defiant. Git! He lowers one of the pistols and fires a shot that nicks the dead toe of her hoof. She raises it from the floor, bends her head toward it, sets it down again, and, after a mournful pause, turns to plod slowly, nose down, from the room. Someone fires a shot, she staggers slightly, pauses, then continues on her deliberate way. The rest of the men, emboldened, grab up their weapons and start shooting wildly at her as she lumbers past, following her on out the hole in the wall where the door used to be, shouting curses and blasting away.

He helps the schoolmarm to her feet, feeling tender toward her as before, all the more so as her high-collared bodice has come unbuttoned and there is a sweet powdery smell emerging from the glimpsed whiteness within that unhinges his articulations in a way the mare's assault or any other could never do. Her own hand, however, is like a stiffened claw and is instantly withdrawn, the sentimental mood clearly no longer upon her. Why didn't you shoot that wicked beast? she cries. In the street, he can hear the men doing just that, the explosive rattle of their barrage like a fireworks display, and for the second time in so short a while, a wetness mists his vision. She was trying to kill me!

I dunno, he sighs. I figgered ifn I could calm her down we could mebbe ride her outa here.

What? Leave this town? I could never do that, you fool! Anyway, she adds, glaring with seething fury at the dampness that has crept upon his cheeks, thet aint why.

He says nothing and she slaps him. So hard she knocks his hat off and her own dark bun is tipped askew. Outside, it sounds like the whole town is being torn apart, and inside his breast it feels that way too, for he has beheld the strands of orange curls peeking out beneath the unsettled bun.

And then the uproar suddenly subsides and the men come piling back into the jailhouse, heated up and blustery with the excitement of their kill, a turbid blur before his eyes of hats and hair and noses.

Whoa, sheriff! Yu shoulda witnessed the way thet crazy mare tuck out yer gallows!

Turned the whole bizness inta nuthin but a passel a toothpicks!

Whoopee! Never seed the like!

Obstructin justice, she wuz!

And more holes in her by then than a cribbage board!

She never even tried t'run. It wuz like she wuz plumb heart-sick'n jest hankerin t'cash in!

But it warnt easy! Thought we'd never bring the ole nag down!

Pumped everthin I had inta the colicky critter!

Criminently! She wuz some goldurn hoss!

Course, now we gotta build thet dodrabbid thing all over agin so's we kin string up this onfortunate buckaroo.

Aw hell, we'll never git it done in time, thet damned mare has seed to thet. I say we jest fergit it'n go git drunk instead.

Now yu're talkin, hombre. I wouldnt keer t'put down mebbe jest a jug or two.

Shore, they all agree. Let him go. He aint hardly done nuthin wrong.

No, boys, says the saloon chanteuse, taking the dark bun off to shake her ginger locks loose, one ruby-tipped breast now bouncing free from her undone bodice, yu caint do thet. The scrofulous varmint is broke the lawr and he's gotta pay fer it.

Aw, Belle, he aint but only a killer, hoss thief, cattle rustler, trainrobber, 'n card cheat, whutsa harm in thet?

The sumbitch jilted me, she says bitterly. Hangin's too good fer him.

The men glance wearily at one another, their shoulders sagging. Shit. Yu shore, Belle?

I'm shore.

Awright. Better go rustle up some hammers'n nails, I reckon.

Thet wood out thar's all kicked t'smithers. We'll hafta rip down the stables'n start over.

Sorry, sheriff, says a baggy-eyed oldtimer with a scar running across his bulbous nose from ear to ear like a clothesline for his beard, and now wearing the deputy's badge. Aint nuthin we kin do. He strips him of his sheriff's star and weapons. Better git yer pore fucked butt inta thet cell thar, whut's left of it, and behave yerself whilst we git on with whut we hafta do.

Whutsamatter with him anyhow, deppity? someone asks and they all turn toward him. He's watching her fasten the ruby pin into place in her pierced cheek. And reflecting on how he was never really cut out for the civilized life and how considering for a moment that he might be was a weakness and a flaw in him, a fatal one as it turns out. The jasper looks like a mule jest kicked him in the cods.

It's Belle. Seein her fitted out like thet.

And now that horizon that was always out there for him is there no longer, and the vast horizon of his inner eye has also withered away.

I'm gonna miss yu, darlin. The chanteuse smiles, tucking her breast in but leaving the schoolmarm's bodice unbuttoned. Aint ever day someone like yu comes driftin through.

138

It *is* not *every* day, he corrects her, and goes into the cell to flop down on the bare springs of the cot there.

No, haw! She laughs, they all laugh. Shore as hell aint!

❧   ❧   ❧

He remembers that when the men went out to rebuild the gallows he looked up through his cell window from where he was lying on the cot springs and saw the stars gathered up and set spinning in the sky like celestial dust devils, and he thought: There's a serious storm brewing. For a time then there was a silence so dense it made his ears ache, and he recalled one hot day back when he was out on the desert alone under the blistering sun and just such a silence descended and in the middle of it a great band of Indian warriors came galloping past, riding bareback and without reins, heads high and staring rigidly ahead as though drawn by something out on the horizon that he could not see, their horses' hoofs raising a torment of dust but making not a sound. As they flew past, he saw that their lips were all sewn shut with rawhide thongs and their chests and foreheads were tattooed with mysterious pictographs and the teeth and tiny bones of animals were embedded in their flesh, and he understood that they were galloping into oblivion and carrying the secrets of the universe with them, and that although those secrets were not very interesting, they were the only secrets there were, and he would not be privy to them. In their wake came a raging river, snapping wrathfully at their heels and swallowing up their tracks, and then, as the warriors vanished and the common sounds of the desert returned, the river shrank to a rivulet from which he and his horse drank and they were sick for a time.

And so he was thinking about this when the new silence fell as he was lying there on his jail-cell cot on the last night of his life, and if there'd been any sounds of sawing and hammering to be heard before, they were stifled now by this thick clotted silence and then erased by the sudden all-encompassing roar of the cyclonic wind that followed on, sucking the roof off the jailhouse and picking up the old wooden desk and swivel chair and hurling them at his cell bars, exploding them to splinters that flew at him like darts and arrows, and he curled up with his arms over his head, giving them only his butt to strike at, it being well tanned to leather from his life in the saddle and more or less immune from punishment. The wind brought with it great slashing torrents of burning rain that bit and chewed at him then, with its driving force more ravenous than a pack of wolves, and when the rain had passed the distressed stars fell out of the sky in a shower of meteors that shook the ground and rattled the cot springs, pitching him, stunned, to the floor. And then the dust and earth and busted stones sent flying by the meteors and stirred up by the bellowing wind came rolling over him as though the desert itself had taken animate shape and had risen up against him, and it buffeted him and blinded him and entered him through all his orifices, stopping up his mouth and nose so he could not breathe, and buried him there where he lay. But he is a man schooled to the harsh and whimsical ways of the desert, so patiently he waited out the turbulence (the worst was over, the marm had left him, and she was not even the marm), meditating the while upon the ironies of his extremity—that he was holding his breath and struggling to survive so that he might live another hour to be hanged—and when it had passed he dug his way out and spat out the earth that filled his mouth and unclogged his nose with his fingers and commenced to breathe again as before.

The storm has left behind a noonday sun, shining down upon him now through the roofless jailhouse ruins. His twisted cell door is agape, and his old gunbelt and wooden-butted six-shooter is hanging on a coat hook on one of the walls left standing by the storm. There seems no reason not to do so, so he goes over and buckles it on, and as he does this he remembers that before the men went out (or maybe after) he was visited by a one-eyed photographer, which he took to be an unfavorable sign, or more than one. He was a cadaverous plug-hatted man with a Chinaman's beard, and he was a voluble enthusiast of his trade. He insisted on showing him his sheaf of photographs of hanged men, giving him a poke in his lower regions with his rifle barrel and jerking on his earring when he showed no immediate interest and closed his eyes. It was his studied opinion, the man said, spreading out his samples and compelling his attention, that a photograph of one hanged man has a more melancholical aspect about it than do those of groups, though men strung up in multitudes of a dozen or more not only provide peculiar challenges and opportunities for the enterprising photographist, being less of a stereotype, as might be said, but they also have a way of opening up the foreground to pictorial scrutiny and drawing attention to those who have not yet been hanged. Put another way, one man suspended solo has a single sad tune to play, while a couple of dozen make a whole band of bemingled and crisscross medleys. They say two's company, the one-eyed man went on to say, tobacco juice dribbling down his stringy goatee and dripping onto his photos, adding to their sepia tonalities as he rubbed it in with a long bony finger, but it aint. Lookit these two renegade injuns hangin here: yu aint never seed nuthin lonelier-lookin than thet! One varmint pendin's like astin a worrisome question. Two's like mockin each other in their silly neck-broke dangle and they aint neither of em got nuthin t'say. I sometimes like t'lookit my pitchers a two men hangin jest fer a hoot. Three's most folks' fayvrit, it's a kinder mystery, like yu know whut two of em're doin up thar, but whut about the third? Like as not it's a mistake, like he wuz jest stumblin along'n fell inta the noose. Ifn hangin a person ever is a mistake, thet is. My own fayvrit number, though, is four. Thet's about the most cloud-kickers yu kin string up in concert and see the whole pattern of em, whilst takin in each one of em at the same time, so's yu git sumthin combined of all the others. Mostly, though, it's on accounta my special regard fer gallows arkytetcher. Jest lookit these here pitchers, how differnt they all are, they's so many novel'n wondrous ways'n shapes a hangin four men all at wunst, and danglin four of em together has a way a bringin out the grain in the wood and drawin yer eye t'the empty space neath their ascended boots. Which a course is the whole reason them estimable things git built.

Rifle now cocked and ready, he peers cautiously out the gaping hole where the street door used to be and sees that no boots will be ascended today, his or any other's. The debris of the gallows, wrecked by the black mare, has been mostly blown away by the storm, nothing left in the wide dusty street but a few scattered splinters like frail bleached reminders of some previous resolve. Now what there is of intent can be measured only by the ominous absence of any evidence of it, for nothing moves. Not even the lace curtain in the window above the saloon sign. The weathered wooden buildings, utterly forsaken under the baking sun, look fatigued and shrunk into themselves, a grim dead silence sunk into everything the way drink can sodden a man. But that they are waiting for him out there some place, or places, of course he has no doubt. The moment for it has come.

Across the way the bank doors are hanging loose off their hinges as usual, and though it's about a hundred yards across a wide-open space, masonry's a better shield than timber, and he figures if he could make it over there he might have more of a chance, or at least last a little longer. He exposes himself briefly on the jailhouse porch, then ducks back inside. Nothing happens, so he checks his six-shooter (a single shot's been fired; he reloads it), tugs his broad-brimmed hat down over his brow as though felt might fend off lead, cleans his ears out, and gets ready to run.

There's a kind of presence out there, like a filled-up space inside the empty space that's seen, created by the portentous hour and walled by nothing but its own taut necessity, and when he enters into it, there'll be no way out until it isn't there anymore, or he isn't.

A piece of the jailhouse wall behind him suddenly topples inward, breaking the solemn hush: he whirls to fire, but there's no one there, and then, even as he watches, another piece of wall folds over like a starched collar and, after a creaking moment, slides wearily to the floor with a splintering crash. Yes, all right. Time to go.

He hunkers down, counts to three, and then charges off on a zigzagging run into the street, heart and legs pumping, expecting the whole world any moment to explode around him and bring a sudden searing end to things. This doesn't happen, not yet, but crossing that space seems to take him years, his boots pounding and pounding the dusty arena where the gallows once stood, his hands sometimes slapping it as well as he ducks and bobs, the distance between him and the bank seeming to lengthen even as he scrambles toward it, and he feels as if caught up in one of those endless tribal hunting dances, he the designated buffalo-headed prey—or the mock prey, maybe it's all the same—his churning legs benumbed and leaden now and his cumbersome head weighing upon his neck and bobbing on its own for lack of strength to do otherwise. He's not going to make it across, it's too far. He can no longer rise from his staggering crouch, it's all duck and no bob, his wind is going, his hat's already gone, shot away maybe, if they are shooting at him, can't be sure, what with the blood roaring in his ears, his sight bleared by sweat and desperation.

But then, just as his knees are giving way, he stumbles upon an old buckboard with a broken wheel, which he hadn't noticed out here before but which has somehow made itself available to him, and he rolls under it and from there pitches himself over a hitching rail and flattens out behind a foot-high wooden porch, gasping for breath, his gun aimed at the buildings across the street. He wipes the sweat from his eyes with his shirtsleeve and scans the rooftops, the dark places, the edges of things. Nothing. Same as before. A deathly stillness. Only thing exceptional out there is his black slouch hat, lying in the sun like an objectless shadow, foreboding as dynamite with a lit fuse. He glances up at the dust-encrusted window above him: GOLD! it says in peeling gold lettering. CLAIMS OFFICE. It's an old frame building, not as sturdy as the bank, but it's where he is and the door is agape, its hinges sprung, so he lurches forward and ducks inside.

He sweeps the interior with his six-shooter, his back pressed to the front wall, but the place is empty, thickly coated with layers of ancient grime, disturbed only by his own boot and hand prints in from the door. He slumps back against the wall, his lungs heaving, surveying his refuge. A flimsy and desolate one-room structure with a collapsing ceiling and a plenitude of uncovered windows all around, already pocked with stray bullet holes; he could hardly be in a worse place. On the counter there is a sign, TAKE ONE, but the box in front of it is empty, the cards that were in it scattered and dulled with dust where they lie, as if to say this seam's long since played out. One of the cards is on the floor by his boot, face-down. Probably ought to leave it there. There was an educated man he knew once, a gambler who had made millions on the river and who then had drifted west for richer and easier pickings and had made more millions, until he lost not his luck but his ability to control his luck, and what he told him one night over the last beer he can remember drinking was: If you have lost the feel of the cards, son, and have to draw blind, don't draw. But he does, knowing what card it will be even before he picks it up, a card he's been dealt before. There are some coordinates inked on its face with numbers and symbols he does not understand, but where they cross at the slender black waist a word is written: *SALOON*.

He pockets the two-faced card after wiping the dust off on his pants, thinking about solitude and how he longs for it always, but cannot and even would not have it, and turns to stare out the front window, past the backwards GOLD (the gold paint is an oily black on the inside) toward the old town saloon across the way with its hanging sign, its swinging doors like folded wings, its still white curtain. It's a kind of challenge, a dare, and one meant for him and him alone, he feels, even if the card's been there forever and anyone might have passed by and picked it up. It's also no doubt a trap. Whole nest of them holed up over there probably, just biding their time with wide gap-toothed grins on their messed-up faces, knowing he'll be coming over sure as a fly's sucked to a turd because it's who he is and he can do no other. Well, and what if he could, what if he told them all to go to hell and just got up and walked out of this pesthole? Wouldn't work. Everywhere he turned the town would still be there, the saloon in front of his face like an accusal and a taunt. Taint whether, as an old prospector once put it, but how. Well. That moribund fellow also declared that the good news was that everything passes. Or somebody did.

So he settles his six-shooter back in its holster and steps with measured strides out on the porch and down into the dusty street, not hurrying, passing the buckboard carriage kneeling toward him on its broken wheel and, a bit further on, his abandoned hat, lying there in the middle of nowhere in its black crumpled loneliness (Solitude! a malodorous old trapper remarked one day with a rueful snort: Shore we love it, kid, it's whut decoys us out here, but it aint nuthin but a pipe dream, like findin a mountain a gold or fuckin angels), but not holding back either, no longer afraid of what might be hidden in things or behind them, until he reaches the wooden sidewalk in front of the saloon. There he pauses in that blinding sunlight and he sets his legs apart and he shouts out: Awright! Here I am! C'mon out ifn yu aint too afeerd! His scratchy voice echoes hollowly, as if he were standing at the bottom of a canyon, and that is the only response there is. He can barely speak for how dried out he is, the frantic run from the jailhouse having sucked all his liquids out, so he decides he has said all he's going to say. He proceeds onto the wooden sidewalk and up to the doors, his boot heels clocking on the planks, then steps to one side to peer in the window. Nothing but a dark cobwebbed and dusty murk in there. Busted furniture strewn about, broken lamps and bottles, the old grand piano fallen face forward as if to bite the floor with its sad scatter of chipped teeth, someone's yellow suspenders trailing from a tipped brass spittoon like spilled chicken guts.

He steps back and considers all of this, looks about him. The only sign of life is his own hat out in the middle of the empty street. He has misjudged everything. The town's been abandoned. He's all alone. His shoulders sag and he realizes how tired he is, a tiredness got not only from his physical exertions but also from all the hard thinking he's been doing. Now all he need think on is finding something wet to unstick his tongue from the top of his mouth. Then worry about a horse. Not sure where to go looking for one of those beings, but if there's anything left to drink in town it has to be near to hand. He turns to enter the saloon and the swinging doors fly open and smack him full in the face, send him tumbling backwards, head over heels, into the street. He can hardly see from the tremendous eye-watering force of the blow, but he gets off a shot at the doors even before he hits the dirt. No one there, of course. The doors rock on their hinges for a moment and then fall still. He touches his nose. Yes, broken. Not for the first time. Not a structure made for this country.

As he lies there on his back with that throbbing pain in the middle of his face, he realizes that the town is leaving him and taking the day with it. The claims office, the jailhouse ruins, and steepled church are already some distance off, their long shadows darkening the desert. The bank follows, dragging its doors. The stables and dry goods store. He touches the card in his pocket to be sure it's still there, estimating that it represents all that he has earned from his lonely travails, all else a figment and a haunting, and it but a sign of them. The saloon is the last to go, as though overseeing the general retreat, and when it, too, is some distance away, the lace curtain in the upstairs window flutters briefly as though waving goodbye. And then it is night, and there is nothing to be seen except the black sky riddled with star holes overhead.